Countdown to 4th of July

Dianna Houx

Copyright ©2023 by Dianna Houx

All rights reserved.

No part of this book may be used or reproduced by any means, graphic, electronic, or mechanical, including photocopying, recording, taping, or by any information storage retrieval system without the written permission of the publisher except in the case of brief quotations embodied in critical articles and reviews.

This is a work of fiction. Names, characters, businesses, places, events, locales, and incidents are either the products of the author's imagination or used in a fictitious manner. Any resemblance to actual persons, living or dead, or actual events is purely coincidental.

.

Contents

1. Twenty   1
   -Days till 4th of July-

2. Nineteen   11
   -Days till 4th of July-

3. Eighteen   21
   -Days till 4th of July-

4. Seventeen   31
   -Days till 4th of July-

5. Sixteen   41
   -Days till 4th of July-

6. Fifteen   51
   -Days till 4th of July-

7. Fourteen   61
   -Days till 4th of July-

8. Thirteen 71
   -Days till 4th of July-

9. Twelve 81
   -Days till 4th of July-

10. Eleven 91
    -Days till 4th of July-

11. Ten 101
    -Days till 4th of July-

12. Nine 111
    -Days till 4th of July-

13. Eight 121
    -Days till 4th of July-

14. Seven 131
    -Days till 4th of July-

15. Six 139
    -Days till 4th of July-

16. Five 149
    -Days till 4th of July-

17. Four 159
    -Days till 4th of July-

18. Three 169
    -Days till 4th of July-

19.	Two	177
	-Days till 4th of July-	
20.	One	187
	-Days till 4th of July-	
21.	Happy 4th of July!	195
Afterword		203
About the author		205

Twenty

-Days till 4th of July-

"I just want the record to show that I was against this from the beginning," Grace announced to the room.

"Duly noted," Grant replied. "Unfortunately, none of that matters right now. We have a wedding to prepare for and less than twenty days until our first guests arrive."

"There is no way we can remodel the hotel in less than twenty days," Grace protested. "Even if we had the money to hire round-the-clock contractors, which we don't, it still wouldn't be possible."

"We don't need to remodel the entire hotel," Molly refuted. "Just the first floor and maybe part of the second. That should be doable."

"Just the first floor? The floor with the foyer, dining room, and kitchen?"

"The foyer and dining room are in excellent shape, remember? We should be able to get away with a good cleaning and some fresh paint, something we could easily do ourselves while the contractors work on the more labor-intensive parts."

"What about the kitchen? There is no way we can get that up to code in a couple of weeks. How on earth am I supposed to feed fifty guests without access to a commercial kitchen?"

"You didn't have a problem cooking for almost a thousand people during the murder mystery dinner last Valentine's Day," Molly reminded her.

"Um, yes, I did. I spent days preparing for that, and that was only one night. This will be at least three meals a day for several days."

"Look," Grant interrupted. "Your concerns are valid, and I completely understand where you're coming from. But this is too good an opportunity to pass up. Now that we have a mortgage, utility bills, and contractor expenses to pay, we need any and all income we can get. We simply must find a way to make this work."

Grace sighed in frustration. "What happened to the big Halloween opening we were planning? That date was much more realistic and manageable."

"You already know what happened. An opportunity presented itself, and we took it; it's as simple as that, Grace," Grant replied.

"Evie was supposed to elope," Grace muttered under her breath.

Molly reached over and put her hand on Grace's arm. "I'm sorry; I know you're upset, and I don't blame you one bit for that. Your much-needed break has been replaced with seemingly impossible goals that will have you running around like a chicken with its head cut off. But I have to believe it will be worth it in the end."

"I promise I will help as much as possible," Rebekah said from the other side of the room. She had been working on her computer while the three of them were arguing.

"I appreciate that," Grace replied. "But you don't have any more experience painting than I do. Besides, you barely have time yourself now that you're Ms. Wedding Planner Extraordinaire."

Rebekah beamed at her. "I like that title," she laughed. "In all seriousness, though, part of my job as a wedding planner is ensuring the wedding goes off without a hitch. In my opinion, that includes making sure the wedding accommodations are up to snuff. So, I will make time to help you get things ready."

"I'll help, too," said Molly. "Does that make you feel any better?"

"Not really," Grace mumbled. "But since I have no choice, I will just have to do my best."

"That's the spirit," Grant said enthusiastically. "Don't worry, Grace, everything will work out in the end."

"If you say so."

Grace stayed where she was seated as Grant and Molly got up to leave. Things were moving way too fast for her liking. Right after they had signed on the dotted line to purchase the old hotel downtown, a decision Grace still wasn't sure about, Evie and Jake had informed them they had changed their mind about eloping and were now planning a Fourth of July wedding. Sensing an opportunity, Grant and Molly had volunteered the hotel to host the out-of-town guests from Jake's side of the family. Grace had tried to intervene, but the group's excitement had caused her protestations to go unheard.

Not that she was unhappy about helping out her friend, quite the opposite; she was terrified of letting her down. After what happened to Evie at her first wedding, Grace felt she deserved the absolute best, something she was afraid she could not deliver. Regardless, it was out of her control. Agreements had already been made, and deposits accepted. All that was left to do was try her best to fulfill her end.

"Why don't we make a list of what needs to be done? Then we'll have a better understanding of where we stand and where to start," Rebekah suggested.

"I guess that makes sense," Grace agreed.

Rebekah got out a notebook and a pen. "Okay, let's get started."

"Kind of old-school over there," Grace laughed as she gestured toward the notebook.

"You'll thank me later once you've had the satisfaction of crossing some of the tasks off the list. It's all about your mindset," she replied seriously.

"Should we add life coach to your list of job titles?" Grace asked. She was only half-kidding. The way things were going, twenty-four-seven access to a life coach didn't sound so bad.

"If that's what it takes," she said. "This is important to me too, Grace. I know Evie isn't a friend yet, but she is my first client and one chance to make a good impression in the community. We're in this together."

Grace nodded sheepishly as Rebekah finished her pep talk. "That's why I'm so stressed; there's so much riding on this for all of us. I'm worried I won't be able to do my part and I'll let everyone down."

"I have personally witnessed you pull off miracles under the most daunting circumstances. Give yourself some credit, okay? Even your enemies wanted to stay at your b&b; that must mean you're doing something right!"

"Okay," Grace took a deep breath and let it out slowly. "Time for whining is officially over. Let's get started and see what we can do."

Rebekah beamed at her. "See, I told you you'd be fine. Now, what's first on the list?"

"Molly estimates that we'll need twenty rooms for guests at the hotel, and none of those rooms are habitable. We might be able to get away with fresh paint, new carpet and drapes, and new furniture."

"Okay, the contractors can do the carpet and painting. We can order new mattresses and, if we have to, shop at a local home store for drapes and bedding. Furniture is pushing it both time and money-wise, so we can give it a fresh coat of paint as well.

"I suppose that's possible. We'll have to see what condition it's in; it was so dated-looking I didn't bother to inspect it that closely. Regardless, that's a lot of furniture. Are you sure we'll have time for that?"

"No, but it might be time to ask the community for help again. The kids are out of school for the Summer and are probably driving their parents crazy. This could be something fun for them to do."

"You want to put our furniture in the hands of school kids? That seems a little risky.

"I'm sure there are some adults that could help steer things in the right direction," Rebekah sighed. "I realize this usually requires skill, but in the absence of time, we will have to make some concessions. Besides, it will give the rooms some character since no two pieces will be identical. What's next?"

"The bathrooms," Grace grimaced. "There are two per floor, all outdated and, more importantly, gross. The plan was to remove them and install a bathroom in each room, but there is no way we have time for that."

Rebekah made some notes before looking up. "From a financial perspective, remodeling rooms we plan to demolish later seems wasteful. Is it possible the bathrooms could be made usable with a good cleaning?"

"I don't know..." Grace trailed off. "At this point, we're not even sure the plumbing still works; it's been so long since anyone has used it. The last time the hotel was in operation was in the sixties."

"So, lots of blues and pinks?"

Grace nodded. "One bathroom is covered in powder blue tile, presumably for the boys, the other, light pink. We're talking floor to ceiling."

She pursed her lips as she thought of a response. "We'll have to hire plumbers to address the plumbing issues. Luckily, instead of twenty bathrooms, we only have 4 to worry about, which works in our favor. As to the style and design, we'll just have to play into the retro theme. I'll start looking on some of the online auction sites to see if I can find some vintage décor."

"You heard Molly say the foyer and dining room only need a fresh coat of paint, so that leaves the kitchen. I fear that no matter what we do in there, it won't matter because we won't be able to schedule and pass an inspection in time."

"Does it count if the hotel isn't officially open for business?"

"If we allowed the guests to stay for free, then no. But, since they're paying...."

"What if we just never said anything?"

"If we got caught, we risk permanently losing our license. Our county is very lax when it comes to building codes, not so much when it comes to health codes. Apparently, they don't care if the building caves in on you, but God forbid someone comes down with a case of food poisoning."

"Fair enough," Rebekah laughed. "In that case, we'll have to see if we can schedule an emergency inspection. Maybe that's something Mayor Allen can help with?"

"Probably, but that's assuming the kitchen can be brought up to code in the next two weeks. Again, it's been fifty years since anyone cooked in there. We're looking at a major overhaul of appliances, and that's best case scenario."

"How important is the kitchen? Could we just have Addie and Bea cater?"

"If there's no other choice, then yes. But they're already scheduled to cater the wedding. They may not have time for that."

"Could you cook here and bring the food to the hotel?"

"Again, I suppose I could try if there's no other choice. Honestly, though, I lack the space and the resources to cook that many meals for that many people. The most I have cooked for consistently was around twenty people. Usually, it's less than that," she waved her hand. "I know what you're about to say; yes, I cooked for a lot of people during the murder mystery dinner. But again, that was one night, and it was only appetizer-style food. It took me days to cook that much, and I was forced to store part of it at Galdys's, which is against the rules, but I had no choice."

"Good thing I didn't know that then. I was so mad at you I might have reported you to the health inspector."

"Yeah, good thing," Grace muttered. She had forgiven Rebekah for how she had treated her in the past and even considered them friends, but reminders of that time still hit a nerve.

"What about renting a commercial kitchen?" she asked, oblivious to the turmoil her comment had caused.

"That seems like the most reasonable of the options. I could forgo sleeping for a few days.

"Why would you need to do that?"

"Because the only commercial kitchens around are Bea's and Addie's. And they will be in use during the day..."

She took more notes, her writing fast and furious. "Let's see what we can do with the kitchen before we take drastic measures. If Mayor Allen can pull some strings, we can get the health inspector out first and see what he says before we do any work. Maybe we'll get lucky, and he'll surprise us. Is there anything else?"

"Evie and the rest of the wedding party will be staying here starting a week before the wedding. So, we'll need to plan a menu and ensure the rooms are clean and ready."

"Why is she staying here?"

Grace shrugged. "I didn't ask. She just moved in with Jake a few weeks ago, so, who knows, maybe she wants space before the wedding. All I know is that I need to plan to serve meals here and at the hotel once guests arrive there."

"When will that be?"

"The first guest is set to arrive three days before the wedding. But that could change as more people RSVP."

Rebekah consulted her notebook. "As far as I can see, this looks doable. You talk to Mayor Allen about the health inspector, and I'll make arrangements with the contractors, then we'll meet up and compare notes and see where that leads us."

"Sounds good to me," Grace replied. It was somewhat reassuring to have a plan deemed 'doable' though she still had concerns. Luckily, Rebekah had taken charge, which helped to relieve some of those concerns. With only twenty days to go until the wedding, she would need all the help she could get.

Nineteen

-Days till 4th of July-

"That man has got to be the most insufferable person I have ever had the displeasure of meeting in my entire life," Rebekah said as she stomped angrily into the hotel lobby. "And I'm from New York, so I have met plenty of insufferable men."

Grace put down her paint roller and turned to face her friend. "What man are you referring to?"

"Thorne 'don't you dare forget to call me Doctor' Walker," that's who.

"The new veterinarian?" Grace raised a brow quizzically. "Where did you run into him?"

"I just got back from taking Piper to see him," she replied as she paced back and forth across the granite floor. "The appointment was on the calendar," she explained when she saw the confused look on Grace's face. "I knew you were stressed out, so I decided to run her over there myself instead of bothering you."

"Wow, I can't believe I forgot about that," Grace said apologetically. "Thank you for taking her, but what happened with the vet that upset you so much?"

"I was in one of the exam rooms, waiting patiently, I might add, playing with Piper when he strode in and immediately began complaining. Piper should have been in a cage; she was behind on her shots, I wasn't brushing her teeth enough or bathing her enough, the list went on. I mean, it was insane. Has he ever tried to brush a cat's teeth? I doubt it," her agitation increased with each pass she made across the floor. "Then, I made the most 'egregious' mistake by calling him Thorne, and he absolutely lost it. Went on this tirade about people not respecting his profession and how hard it is to be a doctor to patients who can't speak," she shook her head. "I swear our appointment was ninety-five percent rant and five percent actually taking care of Piper."

Grace stared at her silently for a minute, at a loss for words. Once she recovered, she did her best to calm her down. "First of all, I'm really sorry you went through that, especially since it was on my behalf. Second, it sounds like I need to do a better job taking care of my cat—"

"No, you don't," Rebekah yelled. "You are doing an amazing job taking care of her. She is healthy and happy and, most importantly, loved. This jerk does not get to make you feel bad about being a good cat mommy."

"You're right," Grace said soothingly. "I'm sure Hailey would have said something if I was doing a bad job before she moved. Maybe Dr. Walker was having a bad day? You know how hard it can be for people to accept change. Everyone loved Hailey, and I wouldn't be surprised if he's having a hard time with the community accepting him as her replacement."

"Most of the people I've met have been nice," Rebekah retorted. "If he's having a hard time with people, it's likely because of the behavior I was subjected to earlier. Ranting is no way to win over new clients."

Grace thought back to her interactions with some of the locals over Easter. She had first-hand experience with just how well some people had adapted to the changes happening in Winterwood. Unfortunately for Dr. Walker, some of those people were now his clients. It would not surprise her one bit to learn they were the cause of some of his strife. "I agree that he should not have taken out his frustrations on you," she began cautiously. "I'm just saying there's another side to this story, and maybe we should reserve judgment until he's had a chance to redeem himself."

"Oh?" she stopped pacing and flopped down in the nearest chair, causing a cloud of dust to escape and encircle her pristine outfit. "How is he going to do that? Cause I sure as heck am not going back there to give him a second opportunity to ruin my day."

"Um," Grace tried to stall while thinking of a way to gently break the news.

"Um, what?" Rebekah asked suspiciously. "Grace, what have you done?"

"I didn't 'do' anything," she said defensively. "It's just he's coming over for dinner tonight."

"What?! Why on earth did you invite that man over for dinner?" she jumped out of her chair and began to pace again. "I can't believe this," she muttered to herself.

"He's not the only one," Grace quickly explained. "The farmers get together a couple of times a season to discuss the current state of things or something, and Cole asked me if I would help him host tonight's meeting."

"To my knowledge, 'Doctor' Thorne is not a farmer. So why is he coming to the meeting?'

"Cole thought it would be a good idea to introduce the man to the farmers in a more relaxed setting. Whether well-liked or not, he is still needed in the community."

"Fine," Rebekah eventually sighed. "That doesn't mean I have to be there, though. I can always just stay in my room. Heck, I'd even spend the night wandering around town if it meant avoiding him."

"I was hoping you could help me with some of the cooking?" Grace said sheepishly. "It's going to be a fairly sizable crowd, and as you can see, I don't have much time to prepare," she held up her paint roller for emphasis.

A loud, dramatic sigh escaped her lips. "Fine," she rolled her eyes. "But this crowd better be large enough that Mr., Too-Good for his Britches gets lost in it. I will not be held accountable for what happens if he decides to go for round two."

"Fair enough," Grace replied. "Thank you," she added before turning back to finish the wall she was working on.

"Do you have another roller?" Rebekah asked.

Grace looked her up and down. "Um, you, my dear, are not dressed for painting. While I appreciate your help, it should not come at the expense of your clothes. Clothes, I might add, we cannot afford to replace."

Rebekah looked down at her designer blouse and capri pants. "Do you have any old clothes I could borrow?"

"Yes, but they're back at the house. I'm almost finished here, anyway. How about you go home and start the dough for the dinner rolls, and I'll join you as soon as I finish this wall."

"Okay, but don't forget to give me the clothes when you get home. There's still a lot of work to do, and I want to be prepared next time I come here."

"Will do," Grace gave her a mock salute, then returned to work. After all, those walls weren't going to paint themselves.

***

Cole had arrived at five-thirty to start the grill and was not in the best of moods. Concerned that something had happened, she confronted him, only to be told they would talk later, which had done wonders for her stress level. Nothing like making her worry all evening while she imagined the worst scenarios possible. By the time dinner was over, she was likely to be convinced that Cole either had a terminal illness or was leaving her for another woman. Both were unlikely, but that didn't stop her mind from dwelling on the possibility.

Six o'clock rolled around way too fast for Grace's liking. Cole had volunteered to barbecue ribs and chicken, but to her, that was the easy part. She still had to make the appetizers, the sides, and the dessert. Not to mention, a lot of it needed to be timed just right to be hot and ready to serve as soon as the meat came off the grill. The things she did for the man she loved.

Guests began arriving shortly after six, each dropping off a case of beer or home-baked item on their way out to the deck. Some still had an air of hostility about them left-over from the last time they had come for dinner. Thankfully, Bea and Junior had also arrived and could be counted on to help keep the peace.

Doctor Walker was the last to arrive, looking like he'd rather be anywhere else than there. "You're not going to win over any hearts with that attitude," Grace told him by way of greeting.

"I could be the friendliest person on the planet, and I still wouldn't win them over," he shrugged.

"That may be true, but you're the outsider here. It may not be fair, but it's on you to earn their trust."

"And just who are you to be lecturing me?"

"Someone who has lived here her whole life," Grace stated. "My great-grandparents helped build this town. My granny is still a well-known and respected member of Winterwood. Unless your goal is to be run out of town, I'd be careful who you choose to alienate."

"Duly noted," he nodded. "Are you going to invite me in?"

Grace moved out of the way and made of show of inviting him in. "Down the hallway and through the French doors," she told him. She hung back for a few minutes to see if he acknowledged Rebekah when he passed through to the deck. When he refused to look in her direction, Grace decided he no longer deserved her earlier call to reserve judgment.

"He really is a jerk, isn't he?" she whispered once she was back in the kitchen.

"I told you so," Rebekah whispered back. "It's not too late to hop in the car and leave these guys to fend for themselves."

"I wouldn't miss this for the world," Grace smiled mischievously.

"What do you mean?"

"Those old farmers aren't going to abide his attitude for long. If you want to see him get taken down a peg or two, all you need to do is wait."

They took turns bringing the hot food and placing it on the buffet table near the grill. Once everything was outside, Grace invited everyone to grab a plate while she set about filling drink orders. After everyone was seated, Cole brought the meeting to order.

At first, things went well. They discussed the effect of the drought on their crops and where they were going to supplement their low hay supplies. Then, the topic of their animals was brought up, and that's when the fun started. Cole attempted to bring their attention to Dr. Walker, but the farmers refused to acknowledge his existence, instead discussing ways to get the surrounding vets to agree to come out to their farms.

To his credit, Thorne stayed silent despite the fact it was obvious he was seething at the blatant disrespect. Grace almost felt sorry for him until she remembered how he had treated Rebekah earlier that day. Taking the place of a beloved member of the community was not easy, but his attitude only made things worse, and he had no one but himself to blame for that.

Unable to take anymore, he excused himself and headed back inside. As the owner of the house, Grace followed him, manners dictating that she apologize for his poor treatment. Before she could, Thorne made a beeline for Rebekah, who had been hiding out in the kitchen under the guise of putting the finishing touches on the peach cobbler they had made for dessert.

"I bet you're loving this, aren't you?"

"Excuse me?" she said, her back still turned away from him.

"I would have thought, as someone new to this little podunk town, you would understand. Instead, you seem to have jumped right on their outsider-hating bandwagon."

Rebekah whirled around to face him, anger flashing in her expressive green eyes. "You have a lot of nerve accusing me of being hateful after the way you treated me earlier," she waved the wooden spoon she held at him menacingly. "If you've been treating people even half as rudely as you did me, then you deserve every minute of hostility coming your way."

Thorne took a step closer to her, closing the gap between them. "Did it ever occur to you that I treated you that way because of how they've treated me?"

"Do you seriously believe that's a good excuse?"

He stepped back, emotions playing across his face. "You're right," he said eventually. "You have my sincerest apologies." With that, he turned on his heel and left the room.

They heard the front door open and close a few seconds later, signaling he had left. Grace turned to Rebekah, who looked as confused as Grace felt. "What do you think that was about?"

"I have no idea," she replied.

"Maybe you should find out?"

"Maybe," she said absentmindedly.

What an interesting turn of events. Now, all they had to do was survive the rest of the evening, which hopefully would have a peaceful ending, unlike the last time. A girl could dream, couldn't she?

Eighteen

-Days till 4th of July-

The meeting the night before had dragged on forever. Who knew farmers could be so chatty when it came to things like feed and fencing? It was almost midnight when the last guest had left, and Cole had gone with him, claiming he was too tired to talk, leaving Grace to spend the rest of the night tossing and turning by herself.

By the time five-thirty rolled around, she was thoroughly worked up and ready to read Cole the riot act for leaving her to spend the night worrying. In fact, she was so worked up she left without Rebekah, bypassing the barn and heading straight to the field when she got to his house. When he saw her heading his way, he at least had the decency to look remorseful.

"I know what you're going to say, and I'm sorry," he said, holding up his hands in surrender.

Grace crossed her arms over her chest and stared at him. "Well?" she prompted when he just stood there silently.

"Well, what?"

"What did you need to talk to me about?" she asked in frustration.

Cole hesitated to answer. "I got a call from the highway patrol yesterday," he said slowly.

She blinked in surprise, confused as to where this conversation was going. "And?"

"And they found my camper. Apparently, Valerie took it and drove off toward the Ozarks with it. As predicted, it only made it a couple hundred miles before it broke down, leaving her stranded in the forest."

It was difficult not to laugh at the image of Valerie stuck in the woods, four-inch heels and all, but she managed to contain her laughter. This did not appear to be a laughing matter to Cole, and she was still trying to figure out what it all meant. "So, what happens now?"

"They gave me two options, either press charges and have her arrested for theft, or sign the title over to her and help her register it."

"I suppose your reluctance to tell me this means you've chosen option two?"

"Putting her in jail seems kind of extreme, don't you think?"

Grace shrugged. "One could argue stealing from your ex-husband is also extreme." She looked away, angry that this woman was again causing problems for them.

Cole closed the gap between them and put his hands on her shoulders. "Hey," he said. "I'll only be gone for one day. After that, she should be out of our lives for good."

"I can't remember the last time we spent an entire day together. Why does she get more of your time than I do?" She pulled away and stomped back to the barn. "This is garbage," she muttered.

"That isn't fair," he said, hurrying to keep up with her. "I'm not choosing to spend time with her," he grabbed her hand and pulled her to a stop. "This is why I didn't want to tell you. I knew you'd get upset."

"Talk about not being fair," she argued. "Of course I'm upset. You made a huge decision without talking to me, left me hanging all night while I wondered what was going on, and then sprung this on me at the last possible second. You're going to spend an entire day with your ex while I have to clean horse poo just to get five minutes with you, and I'm lucky to get that."

He took a deep breath and let it out slowly. "You know it's my busy season," he said soothingly. "Once Fall rolls around, we'll have much more time together."

"Fine, I guess I'll see you in the Fall then," she let go of his hand and walked away. "Have a safe trip," she called over her shoulder.

This time, he let her go.

***

Instead of going back to the house, Grace went straight to the hotel. The tears had started once she got in the car, and she was in no shape to face anyone. Rebekah was more than capable of taking care of breakfast, so for once, she would leave it in her capable hands.

Desperate for an outlet for her jumbled mess of feelings, she turned the radio up as loud as she dared, pulled out her painting supplies, and got to work rolling paint on the ceiling. It didn't have quite the effect that, say, demoing a wall would, but it was better than sitting around feeling sorry for herself.

She'd almost finished the small room when she felt a pair of hands on her waist, causing her to scream in surprise and jump back into the arms of the intruder. "It's me," said Cole as he fought to keep them both upright.

It took a moment for her heartbeat to return to normal, but once it did, she stepped out of his arms and over to the radio to turn it off. "What do you need?" she asked once the room was silent. She kept her back to him, unwilling to allow him to see the emotions on her face.

"I don't want to leave with us fighting," he told her.

If she were honest, she didn't want that either. If something happened to him while he was on the road, she would never forgive herself for wasting their last moments together on a stupid fight she didn't even understand why they were having. Her mind made up, she turned around and threw her arms around his neck, holding him as close as possible, relief coursing through her when he did the same. "I don't want to fight with you," she whispered against his neck.

"I'm sorry I didn't talk to you sooner. We've both been so busy...."

"I know," she sighed. "And I'm being unfair about it. I knew you were a farmer when I first started dating you. Your busy schedule is part of the package."

"That doesn't make it any easier. You're not the only one who wants more time together," he gently kissed the side of her face as he held her tightly in his arms. "You could always come with me," he said hopefully.

Four hours in a truck with Cole sounded like heaven. And that was only one way. But there was so much to do; could she really afford to lose an entire day? If the answer is no, then doesn't that make her a hypocrite? "You have no idea how badly I want to say yes," she said. Tears stung the back of her eyes.

"But you need to stay here and work," he stated. "I understand, baby."

"You shouldn't; I was the one yelling at you not even an hour ago about being too busy for me," she apologized.

"It's alright. We're both just trying to do the best we can. What if we agree to take some time off Sunday afternoon?"

She leaned back to look up at him. "Promise?"

Instead of answering, he leaned forward and kissed her, gently at first, his kisses becoming greedier as the seconds flew by. Eventually, he pulled back, disappointment evident in his eyes. "Promise," he whispered as he leaned his forehead against hers. "I'll call you from the road. Maybe we could talk while you paint?"

"I'd like that," she replied, her breathing ragged. "Be careful, okay?"

"Always," he grinned at her, kissed her again, then left while he still had the strength to go.

As Cole walked out the door, Rebekah walked in wearing Grace's old clothes.

"Everything okay?" she asked, a worried look on her face. "You left without me this morning and haven't answered a single one of my messages or calls."

"Cole and I had a bit of a fight, but we're fine now."

"Oh?" she raised her brow. "I thought you two didn't have fights."

"That's only because we never see each other," Grace laughed. "Which, no surprise, is what our fight was about."

Rebekah was about to reply when Evie came rushing through the door, tears streaming down her face. "The wedding is off," she sobbed.

Grace and Rebekah exchanged glances as they rushed to Evie's side, each grabbing an arm and leading her to the sixties-style couch. "What happened?" Grace asked gently.

The last time Evie's wedding had been called off was because her fiancé had left her at the altar for her sister. Grace had never met her ex, Greg, but she did know Jake and could not imagine him leaving Evie for her sister Shelley. Or any woman, for that matter.

"I was getting ready for work this morning and realized that I was supposed to have celebrated my first anniversary with Greg a couple of months ago, yet here I am, planning a wedding to another man instead. Who does that?" she shook her head. "I was with Greg for five years before we were supposed to get married and look what happened. How can I possibly marry another man in such a short amount of time?"

Rebekah pulled a package of tissue out of her purse and handed it to Evie. "I don't mean to be insensitive, but judging from your last experience, the length of time you date someone does not seem indicative of a happy or lasting relationship."

Evie looked at Rebekah. "What are you saying?"

"I'm saying either Jake is the right man for you, or he's not. Waiting another four years is not going to change that."

"How am I supposed to know if he's the right man? I thought Greg was the right man, and look where that got me," she hiccupped with another sob as fresh tears spilled down her face.

"I don't want to seem like I'm victim blaming," Grace said slowly. "But are you truly certain you had zero doubts about Greg?"

She took a calming breath as she thought about it. "There may have been a few," she admitted.

"And do you have any of those doubts about Jake?" Grace inquired.

"No, but couldn't that also be a sign? Jake is everything I've ever wanted in a partner. He's almost perfect, and perfect doesn't exist."

"We certainly aren't relationship experts," Rebekah said, referring to herself and Grace. "But in my opinion, I think this is fear talking. It's perfectly reasonable to be afraid after what you went through last time, but that doesn't mean you should give in to those fears."

"I agree with Rebekah," said Grace. "If you truly want to postpone or even cancel the wedding completely, we will support you, but I would hate to see you give up your dream due to fear."

"Maybe you're right," Evie replied after she gave it some thought. "It's just, every time I think about standing at the altar, an image of Greg shoving me to the side as he makes a beeline for my sister flashes through my mind. How do I overcome that?"

Grace thought about it for a minute. Evie and Jake were planning to have their wedding out at Wyatt and Kenzie's winery, Vines to Wines. A beautiful spot by the lake was set up for all their weddings, usually under a large tent with the typical seating arrangement. But she was sure they would be willing to change things up a bit, given enough notice. Which, in this case, would be pushing it, but hopefully still doable.

"What if, instead of getting married in the tent, you get married on the pier by the lake?" she asked Evie. "There would only be enough room for you, Jake, and the minister, so all the bridesmaids and groomsmen would line up on the shoreline."

"That might be different enough to keep the images out of my head," Evie stated as she warmed to the idea.

"I could totally make that happen," Rebekah informed her. "All I need is your approval, and I'll meet with Wyatt and Kenzie asap to make the changes."

"You know," Grace interrupted. "The sun sets pretty late these days, but if you don't mind a nighttime wedding, you could get married at sunset. I bet the pictures would be gorgeous with the colorful sky behind you."

"Oh, and we could put floating candles in the water by the pier," Rebekah said dreamily.

"And string up lights in the trees," Grace chimed in.

"Okay, okay," Evie laughed. "You've convinced me. I want everything you just said, plus I want the guests seated at dinner tables instead of chairs. Each table should have a flower arrangement with a candle in it. That way, we can go straight from the wedding to food and then the cake without setting up separate areas."

"Sounds good to me," Rebekah nodded. She had pulled a notebook out of her purse and was furiously taking notes as they talked. "This is going to be the most beautiful wedding I've ever seen," she beamed.

"Thank you, guys," Evie gave them each a hug. "This sounds wonderful and is nothing like my first wedding."

"Jake is nothing like your ex either," Grace pointed out.

"You're right," Evie agreed. "I just need to remember that. Losing Greg was hard but losing Jake would be devastating. I don't think I could handle it."

"Honestly, I can't imagine a world where that would happen. Jake just doesn't seem like that kind of guy," Grace replied.

"And Greg does?" asked Evie.

Grace winced. "I don't know what he was like when you were dating, but the guy cheated on you with your sister, married her, and is now expecting at least two babies with two different women at almost the same time...."

"Fair enough," Evie stood up to leave. "Guess I better get to work. Thanks again; I don't know what I would do without you."

They followed her to the door, waving goodbye as she got in her car. "Crisis averted?" Grace asked Rebekah.

"For now," she replied as she watched Evie drive off. "I won't be surprised if this happens a few more times between now and the wedding."

"Is that a sign she shouldn't be going through with it?"

Rebekah shrugged. "I think it's a sign she went through a traumatic experience and needs extra support right now."

"Then that's what we'll do."

Seventeen

-Days till 4th of July-

For the second day in a row, Grace was up and out of bed before the alarm clock went off. True to his word, Cole had called her from the road, but major construction between Winterwood and Valerie's location had not only cut their call short, it extended his already long trip by several hours. By the time he got home, he was exhausted, barely managing to send a quick text before passing out. More desperate than usual to see him, Grace hurried over to the ranch, again forgetting Rebekah.

When she arrived, Cole was still passed out, which caused a minor dilemma. Did she wake him up or slide into bed with him and curl up in his arms? Both were tempting, but in the end, her responsible side won out, and she did neither, opting to let him sleep and see about the chores instead. Max, his adorable teddy bear of a bull mastiff, followed her outside and to the barn, where she found Riley already hard at work mucking out the stalls.

"Hey," she called out. "You trying to put me out of a job?" she joked.

"Hey yourself," he grinned. "I see you're all alone," he raised a brow, ignoring her question.

She looked around, unsure if he was referring to Cole or Rebekah. "Cole is still asleep," she watched his face and continued when he kept his brow raised. "In my haste to get here, I forgot Rebekah."

He lowered his brow, apparently satisfied by her explanation. "That's a shame. I was looking forward to seeing her this morning."

"Guess that means I'm not out of a job," she replied.

"I'm afraid not. In fact, I better get on out to the field before boss-man wakes up and sees me slacking," he handed her the shovel, gave a mock salute, and then took off for the field as he whistled a tune off-key.

Grace shook her head as he walked away. What a strange encounter. It had been a little over a month since Riley had shown an interest in Rebekah, choosing instead to pursue a relationship with the town clerk, Katie. Why he was suddenly interested in Rebekah again was a mystery. Did Katie break up with him? She supposed she'd find out later, the local gossip mill was always abuzz, and it was only a matter of time before she ran into someone 'in the know.'

Thanks to Riley, she was able to make short work of the stalls. She was contemplating what the next item on her to-do list should be when Cole appeared, looking tired and disheveled. Her attempt to play it cool lasted all of a second before she threw her arms around his neck and pulled him close.

"Hello to you too," he said with a laugh. "You have no idea how happy I am to see you," he wrapped his arms around her and hugged her tight.

"Not as happy as I am to see you," she replied. She leaned back and kissed him. "How did it go?" she asked, almost afraid to hear the answer.

"About as you would expect," he sighed. "Even though Valerie stole from me, she still blamed me for all her problems. Claimed I stranded her on purpose as payback for claiming her mother was actually my mother."

"Wow," Grace exclaimed. "That woman…" she shook her head in disbelief.

"Yeah," he agreed. "There are days…"

"Days, what?"

"I know I shouldn't be like this, but there are days when I wonder how I ended up marrying her. Was she always like this?"

"I think it's pretty common for people to feel like that. Especially when their divorce is less than amicable. It's possible she's been through some things that have changed her over the years. It's equally possible she's always been like this and simply hid it better when you were together. Regardless, I hope she finally gets her act together."

"You're sweet," he kissed her again, longer this time, stopping when Max began to bark.

"Looks like I'm not the only one happy to see you," Grace laughed.

Max jumped up on Cole's chest and licked his face. "Guess not,"Cole vigorously pet the dog, his tail wagging furiously at the attention.

"Next time, you should leave him with me," said Grace. "He doesn't seem to like being left alone out here."

"You were busy," Cole shrugged.

"He could have stayed at the house with Ruby and Piper. Those two love when Max comes to stay," she said pointedly.

"Is that an invitation?" he raised his brow as a grin slowly spread across his face.

"Last time I checked, you didn't need one," she replied.

"Then I guess I'll bring Max over for a play date after chores tonight."

"Then I guess we'll see you later," she replied playfully.

He kissed her one more time before heading off toward the field. "Don't forget about our date tomorrow," he called over his shoulder.

"Not possible," she called back. Nothing short of a trip to either the emergency room or the morgue would keep her from their date. Their time together was so short and so precious; she treasured every second of it.

***

Molly, Grant, Rebekah, and Grace waited in the hotel lobby, with varying degrees of patience, for the health inspector to show up. Mayor Allen had indeed been able to help them out by getting a retired health inspector to agree to an unofficial inspection so they would know in advance what they were required to update before making changes to the kitchen. According to the mayor, he and the former inspector were old golfing buddies, which just goes to show, it pays to have friends in high places.

The guy arrived at eleven o'clock on the dot, introduced himself as Doug Pratt, and made a beeline for the kitchen. "This place is so old; it was closed before I became an inspector," he called over his shoulder as they struggled to keep up.

Doug had an enviable amount of energy for someone old enough to retire. "Have you been here before?" Grace asked, surprised he seemed to know his way around a building he hadn't inspected before.

"Once, years ago. My wife and I considered buying the place after it closed down in the sixties. It needed a lot of work, even then."

"Is that why you didn't buy it?" asked Grace, genuinely curious.

He winced at the question. "I don't want to cause no hard feelings, but we passed because it seemed like a bad investment. This town used to be booming. It had a bus line, a train depot, department stores, you name it. But by the time the sixties rolled around, all of that had disappeared, taking the need for a hotel with it. That's why it ended up for sale; the former owners couldn't get enough business to keep it open."

Grace nodded; that was precisely why she had been against purchasing it. Although Evie and Jake's wedding might prove there was a need after all. If, and only if, they were successful at making Winterwood a wedding destination. A one-off wedding featuring local residents did not a business make.

"Kitchen's exactly how I remember it," he said with a whistle.

"I understand it's unlikely to pass code in its current condition," Grant stated. "We need to know how much, or specifically, how little we need to do to get it up to snuff."

"Bare minimum?" Doug asked. When Grant nodded, he took a look around. "All of the appliances need to be replaced. Counters too. These days, inspectors want to see stainless steel; these old Formica tops no longer cut it. Plumbing needs to be updated to this century."

"That doesn't sound so—" Grant started to reply but was cut off.

"Unfortunately, I'm not finished. The wood floor needs to be replaced as well. I'm seeing signs of wood rot which often means termites are not far behind. If there's a concrete slab underneath, you can take it down to that and leave it if it's in good condition. If not, you'll want to put in tile. You'll also need a proper ventilation system, adequate dry and cold storage, lighting, and a food handlers license."

"Is that in addition to the license the health inspector grants?" asked Molly.

"Yes, the health inspector will give the establishment a license. It is up to each individual using the kitchen to get a food handlers license."

"Is it possible for all of this to be done in, oh, let's say, two weeks?" asked Grace.

Doug laughed. "You're joking, right?"

All four of them solemnly shook their heads. Doug stopped laughing. "Guys, I want to help you out, but you're talking about a lot of work here. Even if you could get it done, you can't just go down to your local home improvement store to purchase your appliances. These things take time, and that's not counting the time it takes to get your licenses. There's a reason it takes months, or even years, to open a restaurant."

It was hard, but Grace managed to control her urge to say, 'I told you so.' Not that she was in any position to brag. While it was true she had foreseen this outcome, it had been in her best interest to be wrong. Now that she was proven right, she had a big problem on her hands. In two weeks, she would have a hotel full of people and no way to feed them.

"Do you have any advice for us?" Rebekah asked hopefully.

He ran a hand over his bald head. "Honestly, my advice is to take your time and do things right. Don't get in a hurry and take shortcuts; they always come back to bite you in the end."

Grant stepped forward and held out his hand. "Thank you for your time," he said to Doug.

"No problem, guys. Sorry I couldn't give you the answers you hoped for."

"It's okay," said Grace. "What you said was not unexpected."

Grant walked Doug to the door and then returned to the kitchen where they were waiting. "So, what do we do now?"

"Now, Grace and I consult our plan b options and hope one of them will work," Rebekah replied.

"You already have a plan? Thank goodness," Molly replied, relief clear in her voice.

"I said we have options," Rebekah responded. "Options are not the same as a plan."

Stress made it hard to think. It also made tempers flare and fights among friends erupt. Sensing they were close to one of those eruptions, Grace decided the sensible thing to do would be to take a much-needed break. Making a show of checking the time on her watch, Grace sighed. "Rebekah and I need to head over to the ranch. How about we discuss this over dinner?"

Rebekah gave her a curious look but chose not to disagree. "That sounds like a good idea. We should have enough time to discuss those options before we meet again."

Molly didn't look as convinced but agreed after Grant suggested they go home and nap. Now that she had officially entered her third trimester, naps had become one of her favorite things. Not that Grace blamed her, she, too, loved naps, and she didn't have the excuse of being pregnant to justify them.

"Why are we going to the ranch?" Rebekah asked once they were in the car.

"We're not. I used that as an excuse to get out of there."

"Okay, well, what are we going to do? Molly and Grant will see us if we go home."

"Good point," Grace replied. "I should have thought about that before I made the excuse."

"We should go to Bea's and talk to her about using her kitchen. That way, if she says no, we can cross it off our list of possibilities."

Grace pulled out of her parking spot. "Good idea. By the way," she looked over at Rebekah. "Riley asked about you this morning."

"Oh?"

"Yeah, he was mucking out the stalls when I showed up. Said he was hoping to see you. Have any idea what that's about?"

"No clue. I haven't talked to Riley since Mother's Day. Besides, I thought he was dating that Katie person."

"I thought that too. Maybe they broke up?"

Rebekah shrugged. "Maybe. But what does that have to do with me?"

"Maybe he's realized he made a big mistake and wants another chance?"

"That's a lot of maybes," Rebekah laughed.

"Well?"

"Well, what?"

"Would you be interested if that's what he wants?"

A few minutes passed before she responded. "This time, I want to be someone's first choice."

"To be fair, I think you were his first choice. He just didn't know you would be sticking around."

"To be fair, all he had to do was ask. I don't know, Grace," Rebekah sighed. "Riley is a nice guy, and it's possible I didn't give him a chance, but I want someone who looks at me the way Cole looks at you. Or Jake looks at Evie. There is no way either of those men would have let you two leave without doing everything they could to get you to stay. Riley moved on to the next woman well before my expected departure."

"I want that for you, too," Grace replied. Her reply surprised them both, but it was genuine. She did want Rebekah to find happiness with someone with only eyes for her. Someone who would stand by her instead of abandoning her when times got tough. Everyone deserved love.

"Thanks, Grace."

The rest of the car ride passed silently, each lost in her thoughts. There were only so many bachelors in their small town. If Riley was no longer on the list of possibilities, that brought the number down to one. It may be time to give the good doctor another chance. After all, they say there's a fine line between love and hate.

Sixteen

-Days till 4th of July-

Cole and Max arrived just before dinner the night before, giving Grace the perfect opportunity to pack a picnic basket and get out of there before she got suckered into another stressful conversation with Grant and Molly. She felt a small amount of guilt for leaving Rebekah to deal with it but figured she could hold her own. Not that Grace planned to make a habit of avoiding her friends and business partners.

The trip to Bea's had turned out to be fun but fruitless. Which led them to today. Bea and Addie agreed to meet Grace and Rebekah after church since Bea's Bakery and Addie's Diner were closed on Sundays. Between the four of them, they hoped to devise a plan that would allow Grace to feed the wedding guests without causing a nervous breakdown.

They had agreed to meet at Addie's as her restaurant had the most space. Grace and Rebekah showed up, notebook in hand, Grace nervously consulting her watch every ten seconds. "Relax," said Rebekah. "There's plenty of time until your date with Cole."

"You say that now, but you know how quickly time flies. We'll all get to talking, and next thing you know, two hours have passed, and not only did we not discuss the topic of our meeting, I'm now late for my very important date."

"Okay, Alice," Rebekah laughed.

Grace furrowed her brow. "Alice?"

"You know, Alice in Wonderland? Never mind," she waved her hand. "Didn't you just see Cole last night, anyway?"

"Yes, but only for a couple of hours. He was still exhausted from his trip to see Valerie, so he went home early."

"How did that go?"

"Like you would imagine," Grace rolled her eyes.

"For Cole's sake, I hope not."

Grace held the door open, then followed Rebekah inside. Addie and Bea were already seated at a table near the counter, with a cake and four plates in the middle. "Hey, girls," said Addie. "Can I get you something to drink?"

"Sweet tea, please," they said in unison.

Addie chuckled and then got up to pour the drinks. "So, Grace, Bea tells me you're in quite the predicament."

"Yeah," she sighed. "In less than two weeks, the b&b will be full, and there will be around forty guests staying at the yet-to-be-remodeled hotel. I need a way to feed everybody, but the kitchen at the b&b is too small, and the hotel's kitchen won't pass inspection in time."

"Oh honey," Addie's eyes widened in surprise. "It takes months to get those things up and running. Please don't tell me you actually thought you could pull it off in two weeks?"

"I didn't," Grace muttered. She pasted a smile on her face to hide her feelings. "We met a man named Doug who said the same thing."

"The former health inspector?" asked Addie.

"You know him?

"Oh sure, he's inspected this place numerous times over the years. He's a good guy. I would definitely listen to what he has to say."

"I plan to, but that doesn't solve my immediate problem."

"No, I imagine it doesn't," Addie absentmindedly began to cut the cake. "How many people will you need to cook for?"

"Total? Fifty give-or-take."

Addie winced. "That's a lot. Between my usual customers and catering the wedding, we'll be swamped here. But," she said when she saw the crestfallen look on Grace's face. "We might be able to squeeze some time in for things like casseroles and other easy-to-heat and serve entrees."

"You could always barbecue at the house," Bea said. "If you get a couple going at a time, you could cook a lot of meat at once."

"For lunch, we could do sandwiches and chips," Rebekah said as she took notes. "Hamburgers as well."

"What about breakfast?" asked Grace. It didn't take a crystal ball to show her future was going to be a hectic one.

"If you could help me in the mornings, we could probably make enough donuts and pastries to cover the group. You could also offer fruit and cereal. Lots of people skip breakfast or often grab an apple on their way out the door," said Bea.

"I could help out with scrambled eggs," said Addie. "If you can, set up a buffet and let the guests serve themselves. Then, you can put out a few loaves of bread and a couple of toasters. That should make it easier on you."

Grace looked at Rebekah. "I guess this seems doable."

Rebekah nodded, the tip of her pen to her mouth. "From what I can tell, the biggest hurdle is storing the food. Do you two think using a refrigerator at the hotel would be acceptable? Or are we pushing it?"

"I don't know," Bea replied hesitantly. "You could make an argument this falls under cottage food laws. It's a very gray area, though."

"You could argue that since the guests are paying for the hotel and not the food, it doesn't count," Addie speculated. "Although, if something happened to one of the guests...they claim to get food poisoning or something...."

"That's what I thought," Grace sighed. "That doesn't answer the refrigerator question. Do you think that would be acceptable?"

"It's risky, and you'll want to make sure you have a proper, commercial fridge," Bea said.

"Has the electrical been updated?" asked Addie.

Grace shook her head. "To my knowledge, the only thing the previous owners did was make structural repairs."

Addie reached over and put her hand on Grace's. "I hate to be the bearer of bad news, but that old knob and tube wiring is a fire hazard. There is no way I would install a new appliance without updating it first."

"What if I bought the fridge and stored it temporarily in the garage at home? Would that work?"

Addie and Bea exchanged glances. "Has the electrical been updated at your house?"

"Yes."

"Then that should work. I can give you a couple of contacts," said Addie.

Grace sucked in a breath and let it out slowly. "Thanks, guys. I don't know what I'd do without you." She smiled at her friends, a genuine smile this time. They had managed to come up with a plan. It wasn't ideal, but it would work. Which is more than they could say an hour ago.

"We heard Riley and Katie broke up," Bea looked pointedly at Rebekah. "Do you know anything about that?"

"No," she shook her head. "I haven't spoken to Riley in weeks and never met Katie, so...."

"Hmm, that's too bad. We thought you might have had something to do with that," said Addie.

"Why?" asked Rebekah.

"There's a rumor going around you're the reason they broke up," said Bea.

"Me?" she put her hand to her chest. "Why would I be the reason?"

"Allegedly, Riley has a crush on you, and Katie got tired of competing for his attention," said Addie.

Rebekah's mouth opened and closed a few times. "I don't know what to say other than I had nothing to do with anything. Riley and I went on one double date, and that was it. We haven't spoken since, so whoever started these rumors is wrong."

Grace made a show of looking at her watch. "I am so sorry, ladies," she interrupted. "But Rebekah and I need to get going. Thank you both so much for your help," she smiled sweetly.

"No problem, honey," said Bea. "Glad we could help."

"I will be in touch so we can figure out a schedule," she stood up and grabbed her purse, motioning for Rebekah to do the same.

"I'll text you the supplier information I promised," said Addie. She looked a little startled by the abrupt end to the conversation.

Grace hugged them, grabbed Rebekah's arm, and made a beeline for the parking lot. "I'm sorry about that," she told Rebekah.

"Not your fault. Thanks for getting me out of there. I couldn't tell if they were curious or accusing me of something."

"Probably both," Grace replied. "I'm sure they meant well, but those two are the biggest gossips in town. Don't be surprised if your name comes up a lot more frequently over the next couple of weeks."

"We need a scandal," Rebekah declared.

"What?"

"A scandal. Something to divert attention away from me."

"I don't think it's that serious," Grace replied. "I mean, it's annoying, yes, but not something we need to fake a breakup or something over."

"Easy for you to say; you're not the one everyone's talking about."

"That's because I already did my time," Grace shot back. "Remember last Valentine's Day when a certain someone accused me of being a homewrecker in front of half the town?"

"I've already apologized for that," Rebekah said defensively. "But that proves my point. I'm trying to start over here, build a business and a life; I can't do that if I keep getting saddled with rumors that I'm a troublemaker or worse."

"I guess I see your point. What do you want me to do?" Grace thought about it for a minute, an idea forming. "Never mind, I have an idea."

"What is it?"

Grace pulled up to the house. "I'll have to tell you later; if I don't leave now, I'll be late meeting Cole."

Rebekah reluctantly got out of the car. "Promise you won't do anything without talking to me first."

"Promise." Grace crossed the fingers on the hand hidden in her lap. If her plan worked, she could kill two birds with one stone. If it didn't, well, a couple of people would be mad at her. Either way, it was worth the risk.

***

"I was starting to wonder if you would show up," Cole teased.

Grace made a face. "You have no idea what I've been through," she replied.

"Want to talk about it?"

She threw her arms around his neck and kissed him. "No, I'd rather spend the rest of the day focused on you. I spend enough time worrying about everything else."

"Sounds good to me," he murmured against her lips.

They stayed like that, lost in each other's embrace, until fat raindrops plonked down on their heads, causing Grace to squeal in surprise and run for the safety of the barn. "I swear the sky was clear when I got here," she exclaimed. "How long were we standing there?"

"I don't know," he chuckled. "Long enough, apparently. Can't complain, though; we desperately need this," he gestured to the rain coming down in earnest.

"We still under a drought emergency?"

"Yes," he pulled her into his arms.

"But I don't want to talk about that either. Now where were we?"

"Here, maybe?" she pulled his mouth down to hers, eager to pick up where they had left off.

Minutes passed before the phone rang, causing both of them to groan. "It's me," Grace announced as she checked the screen. "Evie's calling," she winced.

"Go ahead," he said.

"Hello?" Grace answered.

"Hey, Grace, sorry to call you on a Sunday, but I have a problem and I need your help."

"What can I do for you?"

"We just got off the phone with Jake's mom, and well, she wants to come early to help with the wedding."

"How early?" Grace asked cautiously.

"Like, tomorrow early," she replied sheepishly. "I know it's a big ask, but there isn't room at Jake's for three people. Could she stay at the b&b? We'll pay you, of course."

Grace put her hand over her face and groaned inward. "Of course," she replied. "Let me know when she plans to arrive, and I'll make sure her room is ready."

'Thanks, Grace. You're the best."

"You could say no," Cole reminded her. He came up to her and wrapped his arms around her, her head lying against his chest.

"Can I, though? Really? You know how it is around here. If I say no to something like this, word will get around, and I'll get a reputation for hating weddings or something equally stupid. Never mind I'm already going out of my mind with too much to do."

"Evie would have understood."

"Normal Evie would have understood. Stressed out Evie would not. She's already struggling with the wedding as it is. Cramming her into a one-room cabin with Jake and his mom might just drive her over the edge."

Cole began to rub her back in soothing circles. A pattern she noticed he had whenever he thought she was close to coming undone emotionally. "At least it's just one person," he said absentmindedly. "And she'll probably be so busy with the wedding you won't even notice she's there."

"Tell that to Rebekah," Grace replied.

"What do you mean?"

"Think about it, the wedding planner and mother-of-the-groom will now live under one roof. I won't be surprised if Rebekah kills me before the week is out."

"Maybe you should move in with me for the next couple of weeks. For your safety, of course."

"You know I would love nothing more," she whispered into his chest.

"Maybe I should move back in with you. For your protection, of course."

She looked up at him and laughed. "I'm going to hold you to that," she warned.

"The things I must do to help my damsel in distress," he teased.

"Keep it up, and you'll be the one in distress," she smacked him playfully on the chest, her laughter drying up when he grabbed her hand and brought it to his lips, a serious expression on his face.

"How much time do we have before you need to go?"

"A couple of hours."

"Then we better make them count."

Fifteen

-Days till 4th of July-

After she finished with the morning chores, Grace stopped by Bea's Bakery to place an order for donuts and pastries. Now that she had an extra person staying at the b&b, she needed to make sure she could feed them. The 'regulars,' as she liked to call everyone, weren't picky, but there was no guarantee Jake's mother wouldn't be.

"Morning, Bea," she called out when she entered the store.

"Good morning, Grace," the older woman said with a smile. "What brings you in? Ready to make the schedule?"

"Um, not quite," Grace admitted. "Jake's mom is checking in today, so I need to place an order for the week."

"She coming to help with the wedding?"

"As far as I know, yes. I hope she's nice. Jake's not exactly winning the mother-in-law lottery...."

"No, he isn't," Bea laughed. "The way that family behaved," she clucked her tongue. "Well, let's just hope they don't try to ruin things a second time."

"Oh no, there aren't any rumors about that, are there?"

"So far, no. But I wouldn't put it past them. Everyone's talking about how Evie refused to invite a single one of them. That's got to sting when you consider how they pride themselves on their reputation."

Grace snorted. "They should have thought about that before they sided with Shelley. They can't seriously still believe anyone in town has any respect for them."

Bea shrugged. "They're rich, and they've been here forever. People may talk behind their backs, but no one is willing to be rude to their face."

"My family has been here forever too, but that didn't stop people from talking about us. And worse...." she trailed off.

"You're forgetting the rich part, darlin'."

"Figures," Grace laughed.

Bea pulled out a pad and a pencil and began to write down Grace's order. "Speaking of rumors, I hope we didn't upset Rebekah too much yesterday."

Now was her chance, Grace thought. "No, it's just," she sighed and waved her hand dismissively. "Never mind," she looked away so Bea couldn't see the smile on her face.

"Just what?" she asked curiously.

It was obvious she now had Bea's full attention. Her gossip meter ringing off the charts as she practically salivated for information no one else had. "She will get so mad at me if she finds out I told you," Grace demurred.

"Oh, honey. You know I'd never tell a soul."

How she managed to say that with a straight face, Grace will never know. Luckily, she was counting on Bea telling quite a few souls. "Promise?"

"Cross my heart," Bea said as she made the sign of the cross over her heart with her pointer finger.

She made a show of leaning in close and whispering. "Rebekah's worried that the rumors will cause a 'special someone' to get the wrong idea about her and Riley."

"Which someone?" Bea asked in a stage whisper.

"Let's just say he's new to Winterwood and has a 'professional' career." Grace watched the wheels turn as Bea tried to figure out her cryptic message.

"You don't mean?" she gasped.

Grace was about to nod when she realized several men fit that description, the groom-to-be one of them. "Doctor Walker," Grace said, relieved when Bea nodded. The last thing she wanted to do was start a rumor that Rebekah was having an affair with a man already spoken for. That would be decidedly worse than the rumor she was already trying to distract from.

"Wow, it makes sense, you know. Both of them are from the east coast," Bea mused. "Hopefully, she'll help him adjust a little better. Although that's a lot to ask, considering she's new here too. Guess you'll have to help them both."

"Yes, of course." That wasn't where she had planned to steer this ship, but whatever. If she had to fake taking these people under her wing to achieve her goal, so be it. "I better go," she told Bea. "Lots to do before Gloria checks in."

"I'll have your order ready to pick up first thing tomorrow morning," Bea said.

Grace thanked her and left the shop, stopping to tie her shoe so she could watch Bea without her noticing. Not that it mattered. Bea made a beeline for the phone as soon as Grace closed the door. As she watched, she realized there was one little problem with her plan; Gladys. When it came to gossip, Gladys was second to none. If Grace wanted any chance of this not blowing up in her face, she needed to get to Gladys, pronto. Luckily, she was already at Grace's house. Unluckily, so was Rebekah.

Grace hightailed it home, driving as fast as she dared, only to run inside and find six pairs of eyes staring at her in varying degrees of amusement and anger. "Dang, I really thought Addie would be the first person Bea called," she said by way of explanation.

"She knows better than that," Gladys sniffed.

"I thought we agreed you wouldn't do anything without talking to me first," Rebekah said through gritted teeth.

"I saw an opportunity, so I took it," Grace said apologetically.

"An opportunity to lie?"

"Is it really a lie? I'm pretty sure I saw a spark the other day."

"I'm going to kill you," Rebekah exclaimed.

"Girls!" Gladys called out, her tone of voice commanding their attention. "What is going on?"

"I told Grace I was worried about the rumors going around that I broke up Riley and Katie, so she, unbeknownst to me, decided to start a rumor that I'm dating Doctor Horrible instead."

"Hey, isn't he a character on youtube?" exclaimed Emilio. "I love him!"

"I thought it was a movie?" Grace said, confused.

"Does it matter?" Rebekah yelled. She turned to face Grace. "I asked you to help me, not make things worse."

"How is it worse? If you're dating Thorne, you can't be held responsible for Riley and Katie," Grace reasoned.

"Unless people decide I'm dating both of them and stringing them along," she retorted.

Grace looked to Gladys for help. "Are people thinking that?"

Gladys shrugged. "Not right now, but I suppose it's a possibility."

"Is there anything you can do to make sure that doesn't happen?"

"Ooh, I know," Molly interjected. "We can say that Riley realized how much he cared about Rebekah once he found out about her and Thorne, so he dumped Katie to try to win her back!"

"Why is my life turning into a soap opera," Rebekah moaned. "I never thought I would long for the days of anonymity, yet here I am."

"I, for one, think that's a great plan," Gladys enthused. She turned to Rebekah. "Don't worry; this will all blow over once we get closer to Evie's wedding."

"Then why are we even doing this? If I had known I only needed to ride this out a week or two, I would have never cared in the first place."

"The town is easily distracted, but its memory is long. It never hurts to get ahead of these things," Gladys warned. "Especially when you're new and trying to make a place here."

"This is so embarrassing. What am I supposed to do when Thorne finds out?"

"Act innocent," Grace stated.

"Not much of an act when it's the truth," Rebekah retorted.

"Then it should be easy," Grace shrugged.

"Don't think you're out of the dog house, missy. I have every intention of blaming you when Thorne comes around and trust me, he will come around. His type always does."

"I will happily take the fall," Grace smiled.

***

The day passed without incident, lulling Grace into a false sense of security. She was about to brag to Rebekah when a thunderous banging sounded on the front door. Concerned, she went to answer it, hoping everything was alright.

As soon as she opened the door, Thorne pushed his way inside, heading straight for the dining room where Rebekah just so happened to be working at the table. "Can someone please explain to me why there's a rumor going around that we're dating?" he asked her.

Without looking up from the computer screen, Rebekah pointed at Grace.

"I can explain," Grace said, her earlier show of bravado wavering in the face of actual confrontation.

"Well?" he said, crossing his arms over his chest.

"My boyfriend's bigger than you," she blurted out. Embarrassment colored her cheeks as Thorne merely raised a brow, and Rebekah let out an unladylike snort. "Well, he is," she said defensively.

"I am well aware of who your boyfriend is," he rolled his eyes. "And while I may not wish to go one-on-one with him in a boxing ring, I highly doubt this is a fight-to-the-death over your honor kind of occasion."

He was right. Cole would defend her, of course, but he was more likely to be disappointed in her in private. "I thought it would help both of your reputations," she finally admitted. It was only half of the truth, but it was the truth all the same.

"I'm not sure why you thought that, but it seems to have worked," he said.

Rebekah's head popped up at his admission. "What do you mean? Worked how?"

"I had more patients in one day than I've had the entire time I've been here. Admittedly, many of them appeared to have shown up out of curiosity, but a lot of pets were able to get proper veterinarian care because of this."

"So you're not mad?" Grace asked hopefully.

"I'm confused, but no, I'm not mad. Some guy named Riley might be, though."

Grace winced. Riley was an unfortunate casualty in her quest to find Rebekah Mr. Right. She would have to find a way to make it up to him. Luckily, he was a man, and men tended to fare a little better in the gossip mill. "What do we do now?" she asked them.

"Nothing, right?" asked Rebekah. "According to Gladys, this will all blow over in a couple of weeks."

"The thing is," Thorne said to her. "I can't afford for this to 'blow over.' At least not until I've established a relationship with the folks in the community."

"I don't see how that's my problem."

"But aren't you trying to do the same thing?" Grace asked innocently. If looks could kill, Grace would definitely be dead.

"Even so, what exactly are you suggesting? That we pretend to date until everyone knows and loves us?" When

Thorne nodded, Rebekah continued. "How long would that even take? What if it never happened? What if our 'break-up' caused more damage to our reputations than we're facing now?"

Thorne held up his hand to stop her. "Whoa, that's a lot of questions. Look, no one's saying we have to move in together or get married. All we need to do is be seen out and about a few times. When it's time, we can quietly go our separate ways, and no one will be the wiser."

"I don't know," she shook her head. "I'm trying to avoid looking like the bad guy."

"How do you think it'll look if we aren't seen together?"

"Are you threatening me?"

"For Pete's sake, no, I am not threatening you. I am just trying to point out that the rumors will get worse before they get better if we don't play along."

"He's right," said Grace. "Right now, people think you're dating Thorne. If you don't 'date' him, it'll be back to you breaking up Riley and Katie, only now it will be worse."

"They'll think I'm playing them," Rebekah sighed. "This is so unfair. Although, I guess I have it coming. This is my punishment for Valentine's Day, isn't it?"

"What happened on Valentine's Day?" asked a confused Thorne.

"Nothing," Grace told him. "And no, this is not a punishment," she told Rebekah. "We've all fallen victim to the gossip mill before. Yes, it's unfair, but there are drawbacks to small-town life, and this is one of them. All you need to do is ride it out, and before you know it, you'll be gossiping right along with the rest of them."

"I am never going to do that," Rebekah protested. "People have a right to privacy, and I will never violate that. Especially not after this."

"Look, I know we got off on the wrong foot, but I promise I'm not that bad to be around. Who knows, we might even have fun together," he said cheerfully.

"I guess," she agreed, but she still looked uncertain.

"At the very least, I'll take you to some nice restaurants. Are there some nice restaurants to take you to?" he asked.

"There's a few up in the city," Grace said helpfully.

"Perfect," he smiled. "Is it a date?" he asked Rebekah.

"Yeah, it's a date. I should warn you, though, I'm in the middle of my first job as a wedding planner, so my time is pretty limited."

"Maybe your first date could be at Addie's for breakfast," said Grace. "Everyone who's anyone will see you there."

"Tomorrow morning?" asked Thorne.

"Pick me up at eight," Rebekah replied.

Once Thorne had left, Rebekah turned to Grace. "I would sleep with one eye open tonight."

"Come on, is he really that bad? He seemed kind of charming to me."

"Then maybe you should date him."

"I would if I wasn't already dating Cole."

"Really?" she raised her brow.

"Why not," Grace shrugged. "He's our age, handsome, has a good job, and is presumably good with animals. You won't find any better around here. Maybe not anywhere."

"Hmm," she replied before turning back to the computer.

Grace wasn't sure, but that sounded like a good hmm. Maybe all Rebekah needed was a fresh perspective. Or maybe this would blow up in her face, and everyone would end up mad at her for sticking her nose where it didn't belong. For now, she was going with the first one. There was plenty of time to worry about the latter.

Fourteen

-Days till 4th of July-

Rebekah was still getting ready when Thorne arrived, so Grace took it upon herself to entertain him while he waited. "Got another busy day ahead?" she asked.

"Actually, I do. It's crazy how much power one little rumor can have. Scary if you think about it."

"Something to remember next time we hear something negative about someone," Grace pointed out.

"Definitely," he looked around the dining area as if noticing it for the first time. "This is a really nice house," he said. "Rebekah lives here with you?"

Fully aware of how sensitive this topic of conversation was for Rebekah, Grace decided to shut it down now. "She helps me run the b&b, so it makes sense for her to live here. Besides, how easy was it to find housing when you moved here?"

"Fair enough," he replied. "This town does seem to be experiencing a shortage regarding rental properties."

"And with the housing market where it is...." Grace trailed off, sure he knew just how much the price of houses had increased in the last few years.

"Don't get me started," he grumbled. "Even in a small town like this, houses cost four times as much as you'd expect. It's ridiculous."

Rebekah, having finally picked an outfit for her date that wasn't a date, entered the room. "Good morning," she said hesitantly. "Everything okay in here?"

"We're good," Grace smiled. "Thorne and I were just discussing the housing market."

"Oh," she crinkled her nose. "I'm going to have the win the lottery before I'll be able to afford a house. And I don't play the lottery, so there goes that!"

"You and me both," Thorne replied. "Well," he cleared his throat. "Are you ready to go?"

"Ready as I'll ever be." She looped her arm in Thorne's proffered one.

"You two have fun," Grace waved cheerily. She couldn't help but notice a lot less hostility in the face Rebekah made at her. Maybe the ice had already started to melt? She could only hope.

Jake's mother, Gloria, came in as Thorne and Rebekah went out. "Good morning," Grace greeted her. "I was just about to start breakfast. Do you have any requests?"

"No need; I just got back from having breakfast with Evie," she replied. She looked over her shoulder at the front door. "There seems to be an awful lot of coming and going around here."

Grace hesitated to respond, unsure if the comment was an observation or a passive-aggressive complaint. "It is a bed and breakfast," Grace said slowly. "There are also a number of people that live here, as well as those that come and go throughout the day either for meals or work."

Gloria raised her brow. "And does that list include those sneaking in at five thirty in the morning?"

It took a moment for Grace to understand what she was referring to. "I believe that was me you heard this morning," she began. "But I was not 'sneaking in'; I was leaving." So much for the mother-in-law lottery, Grace thought uncharitably. Who did this woman think she is accusing Grace of sneaking around like a naughty schoolgirl. She was twenty-five, for Pete's sake. She didn't need anyone's permission to come and go in her own home.

"And what, may I ask, were you doing at five-thirty in the morning?"

"I clean out the horse stalls at one of the local farms. I also haul water out to the field for the cows." She left out the part that it was her boyfriend's farm.

"Oh," she said, momentarily pacified.

"I apologize if I woke you," Grace said politely. The woman was a paying customer; despite her rudeness, trying to keep her happy was still necessary. "I will try to be more quiet in the future."

Gloria gave her a curt nod. "Was that the wedding planner that just left?" she asked, agitated again? "Seems a bit unprofessional to be dating during working hours."

The saying 'no good deed goes unpunished' really is true. Here she was, allowing this woman to arrive an entire week early, and did she appreciate it? No, of course, she didn't. "Rebekah is working," Grace explained patiently. "Since it isn't necessary for her to have a dedicated office, she meets customers wherever they feel most comfortable."

"That is definitely unprofessional," Gloria grumbled.

Grace shrugged. "She's a wedding planner, not a lawyer. Although there is that movie about a lawyer who works out of his car, so...."

"Fine," she said in a tone that implied things were anything but. "I will wait until she gets back to meet with her. In the meantime, I would like to know why Evie's family is not involved in the wedding?"

Her eyes widened at the unexpected question. There was no way she was getting involved in that. Wild tigers couldn't pry the information out of her. "Evie would be a much better person to ask than me," Grace said firmly.

"I did ask her but did not receive a satisfactory answer. Family is very important to us. I need to make sure my son is marrying someone who shares his values."

"Jake is fully aware of the circumstances regarding Evie's family. If he shares your values and is still willing to marry Evie, then it stands to reason that she also shares them."

It was hard to read the emotions on her face. Gloria was clearly a woman used to getting what she wanted. Grace was starting to suspect she was here to impose her will, not to 'help' as was previously believed. She also suspected that Evie and Jake could live in a mansion, and they still would have found a reason for Gloria to stay here. Their lack of space was nothing more than a convenient excuse to get out of rooming with his mother.

"I will take that under advisement," Gloria relented.

It could be paranoia talking, but to Grace, that had sounded like a threat. Poor Evie, she deserved so much better. Maybe once Gloria learned the truth, and Grace had no doubt she would, she would feel sorry for Evie and surprise them all by welcoming her with open arms. After all, this was supposed to be the inn of miracles.

***

Shortly after her talk with Gloria, Grace left for the hotel, eager to escape further confrontations. She was dying to hear about Rebekah and Thorne's breakfast date, but her need for peace outweighed her need for details. So, after checking in with Granny and Gladys, Grace took off before anyone could stop her.

When she arrived at the hotel, she found Grant with a couple of plumbers. "Good news, I hope?" she asked him.

The face he made was all she needed to know. "How bad is it?"

"The sewer line collapsed. In addition, we need all new pipes."

"That sounds expensive," she mused. The pipes were expected, the sewer line, not so much. Although, in hindsight, they probably should have. "It feels like waiving our right to an inspection might have been a bad idea."

"We didn't have a choice. There were multiple offers, including Dot's. Waiving the inspection was one of the few things we could do to tip the scales in our favor."

"It doesn't feel like things are going in our favor...."

Grant sighed and shook his head as if to clear it. "These things are common, especially in old buildings. We'll get it taken care of."

"In time for the guests to arrive for the wedding?"

"We could probably have it done in a couple of weeks," said one of the plumbers.

"Could you have it done by next Friday?" asked Grace. That would give them practically zero time to clean and decorate the bathrooms for the guests, but it would be better than having no bathrooms at all.

The guy cocked his head to the side. "We'll have to work longer days. It'll cost extra."

"Can you get me a quote by the end of the day?" asked Grant.

"I'll have it to you by lunchtime."

"And if we agree to your terms?"

"We'll start first thing tomorrow morning. We'll have to bust up part of the sidewalk as well as the street to replace the sewer line. That'll require some collaboration with the city's maintenance department."

"I'll take care of that," Grant informed him. "Just get me that estimate."

"Will do," the man saluted. He motioned to his partner to follow him, each returning to their respective vans parked outside.

"Should we get more than one estimate?" Grace asked Grant once they were alone.

"Yes, but I had to call five companies before finding those guys. Everyone is booked solid."

"So what you're saying is they're our only option?"

"Yep," he nodded. "And it's very likely they know that."

"So, expect a larger than normal estimate?"

He nodded again. "We should have listened to you."

Grace's head turned so fast she practically gave herself whiplash.

"I know," he said with a laugh. "We've been terrible about doing that so far. Molly and I can get...intense when it comes to projects we're working on. Usually, that works to our advantage, but in this case, I fear we are way out of our depth."

"Your excitement is understandable," Grace said politely. "It's the deadlines that are a bit unrealistic. Regardless, we're in it now, so there's nothing left to do but soldier on."

"Even if that leads us straight off a cliff?"

"Unfortunately, yes, even then. C'mon, Grant, it can't be that bad, can it?"

"We'll see. This is going to set us back a long time, though. We may have to postpone the bathroom renovations for a few years."

"There are worse things than having to share a bathroom. As long as we keep our rates reasonable and make it clear we're the only hotel for thirty miles....."

Grant laughed, some of the tension leaving his face. "Thanks, Grace; I can always count on you to find the silver lining." He gave her a quick hug. "I'm going to run some numbers while I wait for the estimate. What are you going to do?"

"My plan is to finish painting the dining room."

"You did a good job in here," he said, waving his hand around the lobby. "I doubt anyone could tell you aren't a professional."

"I'm not sure I can do all the rooms, but I can certainly do some. That might save some money," Grace said, hope in her voice.

"You think you can handle that?"

"If you give me money for pizza and soda, I could get some high school kids to help me. Be a lot cheaper than hiring painters."

"Consider it done. Thanks again, Grace, you're a lifesaver."

Once he was gone, she took her time looking around. What had she just done? There was already too much to do, and she had just volunteered to paint twenty rooms and the hallways. Was she insane? Clearly, the answer was yes.

On the other hand, it would save them several thousand dollars at least. Money they desperately needed for the new plumbing. The front door opened and closed, the little bells hanging from the handle signaling someone had arrived. Curious to see who it was, Grace walked back into the lobby.

"That woman," Rebekah groaned when she saw Grace.

"Is it too late to get rid of her?" Grace asked. "Could we claim the b&b has termites or something?"

"I wish, knowing her, she'd want proof."

Grace made a face. "How did your date with Thorne go?"

"It was crazy," Rebekah exclaimed.

"Crazy good or crazy bad?"

"Crazy good. As soon as we walked into Addie's, people started saying hello to us. People I've never even seen before. One of the farmers that came to the house the other night even came over to our table to talk to Thorne about making a house call. It's hard to believe that one little rumor made all those people change their minds about us."

"That little rumor proves to everyone that the two of you are becoming involved in the community. Yes, it's silly, but people are old-fashioned around here. They want to know they can trust you. Especially with something as important as their animals or their 'special day.'"

"I guess I can see that. Wouldn't it make more sense if we were dating locals? How are two strangers getting together proof of community involvement?"

"As we've established, there aren't many singles in this town. Even fewer in your age bracket. But, you two dating shows an interest in settling down and staying awhile."

"So what you're saying is people are looking for a guarantee that we aren't about to pack up and move? That's....weird."

Grace shrugged. "Stepford jokes aside, I don't think it's quite as serious as you're taking it. Grant and Molly were easily accepted because they rented an office building, started a business, and immediately got involved with community activities. People trusted them. They're putting down roots, and it showed. Before he arrived, there was a rumor going around that Thorne didn't want to be here. That he was forced to accept the job due to some scandal or something. I have no idea how much truth there was to that, but the community perception was that he wouldn't be hanging around long. Dating you changes that perception."

"That makes sense. My dating him shows people I'm not about to take off for New York," she stated.

"Now you're getting it," said Grace. "No one wants to hire a wedding planner who might ditch them mid-planning. In people's minds, you're less likely to ditch a significant other than you are a client."

"Where I come from, it's the opposite."

"It's probably true here, too; it's just, no one wants to admit it. If I'm honest, I would ditch the b&b long before I would ever ditch Cole."

"Does this mean Thorne and I are stuck with each other?"

"For the time being. Is it really that bad?"

"I guess not. He was charming this morning. It's hard to tell if that was real or an act he was putting on for our fellow diners."

"Make him take you somewhere up in the city. You'll find out real quick if it's an act when no locals are around to impress."

"Thanks, Grace. I think I'll do that."

"Good. In the meantime, I managed to get myself on the hook for painting all the hotel rooms. Any chance you want in on that?"

Rebekah laughed at the puppy dog expression on Grace's face. "Yes, I will help you. Anything to get out of meeting with Gloria again."

"Oh my gosh, I'd paint the entire town to get out of seeing her again."

"You and me both."

They high-fived, then got down to business. It was going to be a long day.

Thirteen

-Days till 4th of July-

"Shelley and Jessica had their babies," Gladys announced over breakfast. "One of them was very clearly not Greg's...."

"Which one?" asked Grace.

"Shelley's."

There was a collective gasp from the group seated at the table. "You mean Shelley was cheating on Greg?" asked Grace.

"Yep, she claims it's not her fault," Gladys rolled her eyes. "Since Greg cheated first, she was within her rights to cheat as well."

"I wish I could say I was surprised," said Grace. "But what did we expect from a woman who willingly slept with her sister's fiance?"

"And agreed to marry him literally right after he ditched her sister at the altar," reminded Rebekah. "That woman is the epitome of classless."

"Is this real, or are you guys discussing the plot line for a soap opera you watch?" asked Emilio.

"Unfortunately, it's real, although I can see why you felt the need to ask," replied Gladys.

"Surely they'll be getting divorced now," mused Grace.

"Who knows? Those two have broken up and gotten back together more times than I can count. It's like they're addicted to drama or something," said Gladys.

"That's exactly what they're addicted to," Rebekah replied. "That's why Greg never officially broke up with Evie. The thrill of getting caught is what kept the affair going. Once they lost that, they had to seek out new thrills. Hence them cheating on each other."

"Well, I, for one, hope they grow up. It was bad enough when only adults were involved. Now that there are children, it's time for them to stop being selfish and put their kids' needs first," said Grace.

"Does this mean I'm off the hook?" asked Rebekah.

"What do you mean?" asked Gladys.

"Surely my name is the furthest from everyone's minds now that they have new gossip to discuss."

"I wouldn't count on that. We're trying to help you establish yourself and your new business. The last thing you need is to be lumped into a group with Shelley and Greg."

Rebekah's head reared back as if she'd been slapped. "Surely people would never...."

Gladys shrugged. "All I'm saying is better safe than sorry."

"How will this affect Evie?" asked Grace as she attempted to change the subject. "I'd hate to see her big day, once again, overshadowed by her sister."

"I'd like to know the answer to that as well," Gloria said from the doorway. "Is this the big secret about Evie's family everyone has been keeping from me?"

Grace looked to Granny and Gladys for help. She had always known the proverbial cat would get let out of the bag; she just never thought she would be the one responsible for it.

"I was unaware this was considered a secret," Gladys said slowly. "Can you really blame Evie for cutting ties with her family after what you just heard?"

"No, but I can blame my son for getting involved with a family that clearly has no morals. Evie seems nice enough, but the apple rarely falls far from the tree."

"That's not fair," said Grace. "Evie is nothing like her family. If she was, she never would have cut ties in the first place. Please don't punish her for something she has nothing to do with."

"It figures you would say that. You are, after all, the same woman sneaking around all hours of the night. I wouldn't be surprised to find out you're involved in this mess somehow."

Grace's mouth widened in shock. A million retorts ran through her mind, but none would come out. She was just about to get up and leave when Granny startled them all by standing up so fast her chair tipped over behind her.

"Now see here," she said to Gloria. "This is my house, and I will not tolerate you speaking to my granddaughter like that. As far as I'm concerned, you're no better than Evie's family. I don't care how much money you paid to stay here; you are no longer welcome in my home," she turned to Grant. "Young man, please see that this woman is removed from my property."

"You-you can't do that," Gloria sputtered. "Where will I stay?"

"There are several hotels about thirty minutes from here," Molly replied.

"You will regret this," she spun on her heel and left the room, Grant following behind.

Tears stung the back of Grace's eyes as she stood up to hug her granny. "Thank you," she said as she wrapped her arms around the woman.

"I'm sorry I had to do that," Granny said as she patted Grace's back. "But I've had enough of sitting back and allowing these strangers to come into our home and insult you. You don't deserve it, and there is no amount of money worth the abuse you've felt forced to take."

"Most of our guests have been nice," she sniffled.

"Thankfully. Those that are will be allowed to stay. But, from now on, those who aren't will be made to leave." Granny addressed Molly. "I'm sorry. I realize this might be bad for business, for I did not sign up to see my granddaughter treated poorly."

"No need to apologize, Granny," Molly assured her. "I completely agree with you. The world has come to understand that there is a certain kind of customer out there. We should have no problem refuting negative reviews."

"Glad to hear it. Now, if you'll excuse me, I've had all the excitement I can handle."

Grace helped Granny and Gladys to Granny's room and got them settled to watch their favorite morning game show. The dining room was still silent when she returned. "I'm sorry," she said to everyone.

Molly shook her head. "I'm the one who should be sorry. I should have spoken up long before Granny was forced to.

What good is being a tough broad from Boston if all I do is sit back and watch as my friend gets abused."

"It's par for the course in the service industry."

"That may be true, but that doesn't make it acceptable. Anyways, I think the two of you better see Evie before Gloria does."

"She's going to fire me," Rebekah moaned.

"You had nothing to do with it," Grace assured her. "But she'll probably cancel their reservations here and at the hotel. That's a lot of business we're about to lose."

Fresh tears stung her eyes at the thought. While she appreciated her granny standing up for her, they needed the money. She was not so weak she couldn't handle the occasional insult. Hadn't she proved that when Valerie stayed there?

"Let's not get ahead of ourselves, okay," said Molly. "We'll panic when we have a reason to panic."

Too emotional to speak, Grace nodded in response. When Rebekah grabbed her hand to lead her to the car, she hung on for dear life. Cole was right; she should have said no. In the future, she would listen to her gut, reputation be danged. Grace shook her head; who was she kidding? No was not a word in her vocabulary.

***

Gloria was still at the house when Rebekah and Grace left, giving them a head start. "Maybe we should call Evie and ask her to meet us at the hotel," said Grace. "That should give us some extra time to explain before Gloria finds us."

"I don't think that will be necessary," Rebekah replied. Since Grace was in no shape to drive, Rebekah had volunteered.

"You don't? Why not?"

"Because Gloria isn't going to see Evie; she's going to make a beeline for Jake. Likely to try and use this as an excuse to call off the wedding."

Grace gasped. "Oh my gosh, that's so much worse than Evie canceling the reservations. I don't want to be responsible for Jake calling off the wedding," Grace sobbed.

Rebekah pulled into a parking spot in front of Evie's salon. "Look, you have got to stop accepting responsibility for things you did not do. If Gloria manages to convince Jake to call off the wedding, then that's on him, not you."

"But I kicked his mother out of the house."

"His mother, who was insulting both you and Evie. Even if she hadn't been kicked out, she still would have tried to get Jake to cancel the wedding over the Greg and Shelley nonsense."

"I guess you're right," Grace relented. "But I'm responsible for that too," she whined.

"No, you're not," Rebekah sighed. "Gladys is, remember? She's the one who told us about Shelley and the baby in the first place. Regardless, the whole town is talking about it. It was only a matter of time before Gloria found out anyway."

Grace pulled a tissue packet from the glove compartment and blew her nose. "Okay, I'm ready," she said.

As soon as they entered the salon, Grace burst into tears. Stunned, Evie rushed toward her, grabbed her hand, and led her back to the employee break room.

"What on earth!" she exclaimed.

Since Grace could not control herself, Rebekah explained the earlier events. When she was done, Evie looked horrified.

"I am so sorry," she said to Grace. "We knew she would be a handful, but we never expected her to behave like that."

Those few words confirmed Grace's previous suspicions. "I'm sorry," Grace said. "Rebekah thinks she'll go straight to Jake and try to convince him to call off the wedding."

"Yeah, that's exactly what she'll do."

"Aren't you concerned?" Grace asked a calm and collected Evie.

"No, why would I be?"

"Because that's his mother," Grace said as if it were obvious.

Evie laughed and placed her hand on Grace's arm. "If Jake is willing to leave me over his mother's actions, I don't want to be with him. I, however, have zero concerns that he'll do that. He knows what his mother is like. He'll humor her outburst, and then he'll set her up in the nearest hotel."

"You could have saved me the hassle and done that in the first place," Grace pouted.

"You're right, and we should have. But she insisted on being close by and, at the time, it seemed pointless to argue."

"Sounds like our crisis has been averted," Rebekah informed Grace. "How about we take our minds off this and go do some painting?" she exclaimed, as if offering Grace a trip to the beach instead of a day of hard labor.

"Will you let us know what happens with Jake?" Grace asked Evie.

Evie held up her pinkie and locked it with Grace's. "Pinkie swear," she smiled.

"Okay then, off we go," she said to Rebekah.

When they arrived, the plumbers were hard at work, which meant Grant had accepted their estimate. Hopefully, it wasn't as bad as they had expected; she would have to remember to ask him about it later.

Just as she was about to start on one of the downstairs bedrooms, one of the plumbers popped in to talk to her. "We just discovered there's no access point to the plumbing in the upstairs bathrooms," he informed her.

Grace stared at him blankly. "What does that mean?"

"It means we will either have to tear out the floor or we'll have to tear out the ceiling to replace the pipes."

"Th-that sounds bad," she stammered. Could this day get any worse? Why did she ask that? Every time she asked that, the answer was always yes.

"It's not ideal, but it is common in these old buildings. Since it was built before plumbing, all of it was retrofitted. Unfortunately, most people built walls and bulkheads around the pipes, forgetting they might need to access them again one day."

"Which would be the least amount of work?"

"The floor would be easier, but we'd have to rip out the tile, which you would then have to replace. Since you're worried about time, I suggest the ceiling, though it will cost a little bit more since it will be harder to access."

She should check with Grant, but they didn't have time for her to run to him every time they had a problem. Which was likely to be often the rate things were going. "Go ahead and go with the ceiling. Will this affect my ability to paint?"

"It shouldn't. The second-floor bathrooms are right above the first-floor ones."

"Okay, thanks for letting me know."

Back in the bedroom, she pulled out her phone and sent Grant a quick update. That done, she grabbed a paintbrush and got to work, praying all the while the day did not, in fact, get worse.

Twelve

-Days till 4th of July-

"Any updates from the rumor mill?" Grace asked Gladys when she appeared in the dining room. She was almost afraid to hear the answer but figured it was better to know so she could prepare.

Gladys began to slowly walk around the dining room table. "My new hip gets a little creaky when I sit for too long," she explained when Grace gave her a curious look. "Anyway, according to my sources, Greg and Shelley are over for good."

"For real this time?" Grace asked suspiciously. Greg and Shelley had broken up and gotten back together so many times in the last year it was hard to believe this time would be any different.

"Greg spent the day packing Shelley's things and dropped them off at her folk's house."

"Wait, isn't she still in the hospital?"

"Yep, Greg wasted no time getting her out of their place once he realized the baby wasn't his. Wasted no time running around town claiming to be the victim too."

"You're kidding!" Grace exclaimed. "Did he forget what he did to Evie? Or that his mistress is in the room next door to his wife with his baby?"

"He claims none of that was his fault; it was all Shelley. Is trying to paint her as some kind of femme fatale or something," she waved her hand dismissively.

"That guy is a piece of work. Please tell me no one's buying this garbage."

"No, which is only making him whine louder. He tried to go to the bar last night looking for sympathy and discovered he was still denied service. Sat outside the establishment crying to everyone who passed by until the owner called the police and had him run off."

"Surely he didn't think Cole and Jake would let him into their bar? Has he completely lost his mind?"

"I'm talking about the other bar," she explained.

"Tom's?"

Gladys nodded as she continued her laps. "Tom was on duty the day Evie came in in her wedding dress and told everyone what Greg had done. He's been persona non grata ever since."

"Wow, someone needs to tell Evie that. She's been too ashamed to show her face there since it happened. I bet knowing she had their support would mean a lot to her."

"Everyone supported that child," Gladys clucked. "Everyone but her family, that is. Cole refused to serve him too, long before Jake became part owner in his bar."

Grace nodded. "That I expected. Any other news?"

"Let's see," Gladys paused to think. "Greg plans to move Jessica and the baby in as soon as they leave the hospital, Riley and Katie are back together, and Gloria is running around, causing a stink about getting kicked out of here."

The last part caused her to momentarily stop kneading the dough she was working on. "How are people reacting to that?" she asked hesitantly. Did she really want to know?

"You are just as much a child of this town as Evie is," Gladys scolded gently. "No one is going to take the side of some random woman over you. So don't worry about that."

That was reassuring, although she still had some detractors. Even though Dot was gone, a few older folks were still around who didn't care much for her business endeavors. It would really suck if they could use this incident with Gloria to further their agenda.

"What's the story with Katie and Riley?" she asked, changing the subject.

"Allegedly, now that Rebekah is dating Thorne, Katie no longer feels threatened by her, so she decided to get back together with Riley."

"And Riley agreed?"

At that, Gladys stopped walking. "I don't know," she said. "Riley is one of the few people in town I'm unable to get information on."

"Why is that?" Grace was shocked to hear there was someone outside of Gladys's reach. Her sources were legendary, and no one seemed immune.

"He doesn't come into town," she shrugged. "Same with Cole. Josie and I were pretty concerned when you started dating him for that very reason."

Grace smiled at Gladys's nickname for her granny. "Cole owns a bar, silly. He's in town all the time. Well, during the off-season anyway."

"Bartenders are notorious for getting gossip, not creating it," Gladys explained. "Cole was a complete mystery. Still is outside of the information we get from you."

"Gladys!" Grace exclaimed. "Please don't tell me you're using me to spread gossip about Cole!"

"Of course not," she pfft. "I'm offended you'd even ask."

Grace gave her a look. "Okay, fine, I suppose it's fair you asked," she relented. "But I prefer to know gossip, not spread it. When you get to my age, you'll understand. Outside of doctors' appointments and the occasional outing, my health keeps me cooped up at home. This is my only way to stay connected to the community and its people."

"Aww, Gladys," Grace wiped off her hands and went around the corner of the counter to hug her. "I'm sorry, I've been so busy I've been neglecting you and Granny. I need to get you two out of the house more."

"I appreciate that child, but outings are rough on us. Although, a trip down to Bea's Bakery for a cup of coffee and a scone occasionally might not be so bad."

"Done," Grace hugged her again, careful not to knock her off balance. "I'll make arrangements with Bea when I see her later today. Maybe we can make it a weekly thing."

"Bi-weekly would be good enough," she replied. "Gives us plenty of time to recover between outings."

Grace nodded, then went back to her dough. Two weeks to recover from a simple outing to a bakery seemed like a long time. Were Granny and Gladys in worse shape than she thought? The thought of losing them brought tears to her eyes, and she had to work hard to hold them back so Gladys wouldn't see.

Times like this reminded her just how short and precious life is. And just how much time she missed spending with the people she loved most. It may be time to cut back on work and focus on her family. Who was she kidding? She'd been saying that for months and something would come up every time she thought she could do it. Proof that something would always come up. If she wanted things to change, she would have to be the one to make them change. Starting with learning how to say the word 'no.'

***

Cole and Riley showed up after lunch with a truck and trailer ready to take Grace to a warehouse to pick up the commercial fridge she needed. Rebekah had conveniently needed to be elsewhere, so that left the three of them on their own. To say it was awkward would be an understatement.

Riley didn't know Grace was the one who caused him grief, but she did, which only made his kindness toward her all the more unbearable. There had to be a way to make it up to him, but how did one go about something like that? Did she say, 'Hey, sorry I threw you under the bus and made people question your reputation?' Did she bake him his favorite pie and hope that was good enough?

If he was back with Katie because he wanted to be, then no harm was done, right? If he was back with her because he felt he had to be, that was a different thing entirely. Did men really care about stuff like this? Was she making a mountain out of a molehill? She should ask and get it over with it.

"Heard you and Katie got back together," she said nonchalantly. They were on their way to the warehouse, the three of them squeezed into the front seat, Grace sandwiched between Riley and Cole. If this conversation went sideways, it would make for one heck of a long trip.

"Yep," he said happily. "We had a bit of a hiccup for a minute there, but things are good now."

She looked straight ahead, studiously avoiding the warning look Cole was giving her. "I was just curious since you asked about Rebekah the other day."

"I was hoping Rebekah could help me out," he replied sheepishly. "Katie was convinced something was going on between me and Rebekah, and I thought maybe if she explained to her that we're nothing more than friends, it would put Katie's mind at ease. Luckily for me, Rebekah started dating the new doc, so it's been smooth sailing ever since," he waved his hand as if sailing on the ocean, a big smile on his face.

Relief flooded her senses like never before. Her little white lie had actually helped Riley instead of hurt him. Not that it excused her lying, she would have to live with that, but at least no one got hurt. "I'm happy to hear that," she told him. And boy, did she mean it.

"Maybe we should all get together sometime," he said. "All we seem to do these days is work. Might be fun to spend an evening with a group of people our age."

Grace remembered the dinner party she and Cole had hosted around Easter. It had been a lot of fun and a great way to introduce people who otherwise may not have met. But did she have time for this? Not really. Unless... "What do you think about a painting party?" she asked Riley.

"Like, one of those things where people drink wine and paint pictures of cats or something?"

"Not exactly," she said slowly. "More like, one of those things where a group of people gets together, eats pizza, and paints the walls in my hotel while they laugh and joke around and have fun, but ultimately do a really great painting job."

Cole snorted. "Are you really trying to sucker your friends into doing free labor under the guise of a party?"

"I'm in," Riley said. "It sounds fun to me," he said defensively when she and Cole looked at him. "Right now, anything beats a tractor. Not that I'm complaining," he quickly added.

"Thank you, Riley," Grace beamed at him, then turned to Cole and stuck her tongue out at him.

"Fine," he laughed. "Have your little painting party. Just don't be upset if no one else falls for your little scheme."

"It's not a scheme," she pouted. "I have every intention of being upfront and honest with everyone. You will come, won't you?" she gave him puppy dog eyes, which he attempted to ignore by focusing on the road.

"Of course, I'll come," he sighed. "But this is not the kind of thing I usually have in mind on my extremely rare nights off."

"I know," she said, immediately remorseful. Poor Cole worked so hard, and here she was, taking advantage of him. "Forget, I asked."

Cole reached over and took her hand. "It's okay. Like Riley said, it might even be fun. I just don't want this to become the norm, okay?"

"Okay," she readily agreed. If she were honest, she didn't want that either, so upholding her promise would be easy.

They arrived at the warehouse and pulled to the loading bay, Cole expertly backing the trailer up to the dock. The warehouse worker instructed Grace to inspect the fridge before they loaded it onto the trailer. After giving it a quick once over, she was about to sign the paperwork when she noticed the plug. "What's that," she asked the worker.

He gave her a funny look. "It's a plug."

"I get that," she said defensively. "But I've never seen one like it before. What kind of plug is it?" She felt stupid for asking, especially since he looked at her like she was stupid, but she did not have an outlet in her garage or even the house to accept that kind of plug.

The guy turned to Cole, who had walked over to see what the holdup was. "You know what to do with one of those?" he asked, pointing to the plug.

"Yes," Cole stated, clearly surprised by the question.

"Good," he turned to Grace and held out the clipboard and a pen. "Sign here, please."

It was tempting to refuse. She was more than a little angry and humiliated at having been treated like that, but everyone was busy, and no one had time for her to put that man in his place. Not that it would do any good anyway. So, she signed, then stood back and watched as they loaded it onto the trailer with a forklift. Which brought the question, how would they get it off the trailer when they got home? Guess that was a problem for the men.

Back home, Cole inspected the area in the garage where they were supposed to install the fridge. The 'garage' being a former carriage house that had been 'slightly' modified over the years to resemble a modern-day place to park your car. In reality, it was a glorified storage unit someone had installed a garage door in that contained a few workbenches and outdated tools that one might consider antiques.

"This outlet only accepts two prongs," he said to Grace.

"Yep," she nodded her head and rolled her eyes. "I questioned it back at the warehouse, but hey, what do I know? I'm just a girl."

"Looks like we need to run new wire," Riley interrupted. "This is going to take a GFCI outlet. Where is the box?"

"The box?" asked Grace.

"Your electric box."

"There's two. One on the porch and one in the pantry."

"I'll go check them out," he volunteered.

Cole approached her cautiously. "I'm sorry; I should have taken the time to listen to you. It was hot, and I just wanted to get out of there."

"I suppose I'll forgive you," she demurred. "But only because I doubt there were any other options."

"I suppose I'll just have to make it up to you," he grinned.

Before she could react, he pulled her into his arms and kissed her. "How's that?" he asked when they came up for air.

"It's a start," she replied huskily.

"Just a start?"

"What can I say? My delicate sensibilities were hurt. It's going to take a lot to make up for that." It was hard, but she managed to hide her smile, her lips twitching slightly at the corner, the only hint she was teasing.

"Guess I'll have to work harder then," he pulled her closer and kissed her again, continuing until Riley returned from inspecting the control panels. "We'll continue this later," he whispered.

If only all the times people failed to listen to her resulted in time spent in Cole's arms. A girl could dream.

Eleven

-Days till 4th of July-

The first thing Grace did that morning was create a group chat with everyone she wanted to invite to her painting party. Then, she sent a text explaining the party and talking it up as much as she thought she could get away with, considering it was more work than party. For his part, Riley responded first, enthusiastically agreeing to come and reiterating how fun it sounded. At this point, she owed that man more than a pie. Especially since he had spent most of his afternoon rewiring her garage the previous day.

"What's this about?" Rebekah asked when she entered the dining room. She had her phone in her hand and gestured toward it like it was something undesirable.

"I am trying to convince our friends to help us paint the hotel rooms by dressing it up like a fun party," Grace explained.

"That part I got and think is a great idea. It's the part where you invited Thorne I don't understand."

"He's supposed to be your boyfriend. It would look suspicious if I didn't invite him."

"He's a doctor. Do you really think a doctor will spend a night painting?"

"If he wants to meet new people and continue establishing himself in the community, he will," she shrugged. "If he wants to support his 'girlfriend,' he definitely will."

Rebekah narrowed her eyes. "Is this part of your ploy to get us together?"

"Yes, I purposefully bought an old hotel, prematurely booked a bunch of guests, then volunteered to do all the painting myself, all so I could try to get you and Thorne, who didn't even live here when all this started by the way, together," Grace replied sarcastically.

"Fine. But I still find it rather suspicious that you keep coming up with reasons for him and me to spend time together."

"I'm sensing a case of the 'lady doth protest too much,'" Grace looked away, hiding her smile behind her teacup.

"You're infuriating, you know that?"

"That's why you love me," Grace shrugged.

"Hmmph," Rebekah turned on her heel and left the room. "I'll be out at the winery this morning," she called over her shoulder.

"You'll thank me when it's your wedding you're planning," Grace called back.

She laughed when she heard Rebekah snort and grumble something very likely unladylike. A quick check of her messages showed that quite a few of their friends had already agreed to show up. Since she had scheduled the party for the next night, she had two days of painting to get through by herself. Thankfully, it didn't seem as bad when she knew she had something to look forward to.

Deciding that now would be a good time to check in with Mayor Allen, she skipped the hotel and headed straight for town hall, hoping to catch him in his office. "Good morning," she called to Katie as she passed the clerk's window.

"Hey, Grace?" Katie called out, stopping Grace in her tracks.

The last time Grace interacted with Katie was around Christmas time, so she was surprised to see the woman wanted to chat. Not that they were enemies; they just weren't...friends. Katie was a couple of years older than Grace, so she had been a part of Cassie and Evie's friend group in high school, while Grace had been a bit of a loner.

"What's up?" she asked when she returned to the window she had just passed.

"Um," Katie hesitated to reply, the look on her face one of nervous embarrassment.

Grace knew that feeling all too well, so she took pity on the woman and smiled her friendliest smile. "Everything okay?"

"It's just Riley called me this morning and invited me to some party you're supposed to host tomorrow night. Since you didn't invite me yourself, I wanted to make sure you don't mind if I tag along?"

"Of course not," Grace replied. "I talked to Riley yesterday and told him to invite you."

"Oh, good," she said, looking relieved. "He didn't mention that part, so I wasn't sure..." she trailed off.

"It's my fault," Grace apologized. "I don't have your number; otherwise, I would have included you in the group text. I should have asked; I've just been so busy it slipped my mind," she stopped talking when she realized she was rambling. Something she had a bad habit of doing when she was nervous. Which she shouldn't be. There was no reason a perfectly normal conversation with a woman she'd known for years should make her nervous.

"Is, um, Rebekah gonna be there?"

"Yes," Grace pulled out her phone. "So is Cole, Evie, Jake, Cassie, Emilio, Vanessa, Conor, and Thorne," she said, reading off the list of people she invited. "Grant and Molly wanted to come, but the paint fumes aren't good for the baby, so they're going to stay home and keep Granny and Gladys company." Grace sighed; she was rambling again. And lying. While most of the people she had just named had agreed to come, Thorne had not. And his was the only name Katie wanted to hear.

"Sounds good," she replied, her demeanor noticeably cheerier. "I will see you then!"

"Looking forward to it," she said. "Thanks, Katie." She turned to leave, relieved their conversation was finally over.

"Wait," Katie called out.

Grace groaned inwardly. She had been so close. "What's up?" she asked, back at the window.

"Mayor Allen isn't in his office," she informed her. "That's who you were going to see, right?"

"Oh," Grace said, disappointed. "Thanks for letting me know."

She hightailed it out of there before things could get any more awkward. Back in her car, she debated what to do. On the one hand, there was a lot of work at the hotel. On the other, she still had yet to receive a response from

Thorne. Yes, he could just be busy. But it couldn't hurt to make sure, right?

***

When she arrived at the vet's office, the parking lot was so packed there wasn't a single place to park. Considering the parking lot was nothing more than a gravel lot where people usually just parked anywhere space was available, it was quite a feat to accomplish. Which meant Thorne was busy. Fair enough, but she still wanted to talk to him. So she called the office, feigned an emergency, and got the receptionist to arrange a meeting with Thorne over lunch.

Now that she was sitting in his office waiting for him, she realized just how stupid of an idea that had been. The story of "The Boy Who Cried Wolf" came to mind, shaming her for the second white lie she had told about this man.

"Grace, what seems to be the problem," he asked as he walked into the room. He looked around and then raised a brow when he saw she was alone. "You do realize I'm an animal doctor and not a human one, right?"

She wanted to roll her eyes or maybe make a sarcastic comment, but, all things considered, his question was fair. "I lied," she blurted out.

"About what?" he asked.

His voice held a note of concern which only made her feel worse. "I don't have an emergency. I wanted to talk to you, but you were so busy, and the receptionist wouldn't let me see you unless I had a problem, so I lied," she hung her head in shame, equal parts embarrassed to admit her lie and to realize that she was, once again, rambling.

"In the future, you could just text or call my personal phone," he said gently.

"I was afraid you wouldn't answer me," she admitted.

"Is this about the text you sent this morning?"

"Yes, it's crucial you come to the party."

"Why?"

"Because you need to make friends. And because Rebekah will be there."

"I see. I never said I wasn't coming."

"You never said you were," she retorted.

"As you already said, I've been busy."

"Too busy to send a quick reply?"

"Grace, what's really going on? I don't know you well enough to know if this is out of character for you, but I can't help but feel like it is."

What was going on? Why did she feel so invested in the lives of these people? People, until recently, she hadn't even known existed. Although, she hadn't known Cole existed either, and she would fight a bear with her bare hands for him. The truth was that despite their beginning, she had come to care about Rebekah. To see her as the sister she never had. The longer they lived together, the more time together they spent, the closer they became. She wanted to see her happy. More importantly, she felt she owed it to her.

"I feel responsible," she admitted.

"For what, exactly?"

"For the mess I created. I wasn't trying to hurt anyone, and so far, I don't think I have. But my lie has affected people."

Thorne took a seat behind his desk and pulled out a lunch box. "Do you mind if I eat while we talk?" When she shook her head, he pulled out a sandwich. "I already told you that little lie of yours has done wonders for my practice," he said between bites.

"Yeah, and now you, Rebekah, Riley, and Katie depend on that lie. What happens when you and Rebekah 'break up'? What happens if people find out you were never dating in the first place?"

"That's on them. This was never more than a rumor, Grace. You aren't responsible for what people choose to believe."

"I started the rumor," she reminded him.

"And?" he shrugged. "It doesn't matter who started it, doesn't make it true. Also doesn't mean people shouldn't mind their own business."

"People like me?" she said, shame in her voice again.

"You were trying to help, and you did. If you learned a lesson in all this, even better."

"Does that mean you're not coming?"

"No, it doesn't mean that," he held up his hands when he saw the hopeful expression on her face.

"Don't get too excited. I will come to the party and play my part as Rebekah's boyfriend. But, Grace, you need to take a step back and stop trying to control everything around you. You are not responsible for me and Rebekah. Nor are you responsible for Katie and Riley. I sincerely appreciate your help, but it's time to officially retire your fairy godmother wings and let the rest of us take it from here.

Grace wiped the tears from her eyes. "You're right," she said once she had calmed down enough to speak. "I've become someone I'm not, and I'm ashamed of that."

"It's okay," he said gently. "Your intentions were good." He handed her a box of tissue. "Do you have anyone you can talk to?" he asked.

She looked up at him. "You mean, like a counselor?"

"A counselor, trusted friend, or relative?"

"You think I need a counselor," she stated.

"I'm not saying there's something wrong with you; I just think you could benefit from having someone to discuss your feelings with. I would volunteer, but I tend to be better with animals," he laughed to lighten the mood, but it didn't work.

"I tend to get this way when my life feels out of control," she whispered. "It's like I have this desperate need to claw back what little control I can, even if it means saying or doing things I normally wouldn't."

"You feel like your life is out of control?" he asked, all traces of laughter gone.

"My life has changed so much in the last six months; I barely recognize it anymore. Granny tried to end her life so I would get her life insurance; I opened the b&b, then there was the thing with Hunter and Cole, not to mention all the people in and out of my life. Now there's the hotel and Evie's wedding; the list goes on."

"How much of that do you feel you had a choice in?"

"Cole," she laughed, but her tune was humorless. "Even that seems out of my control. We're both so busy we barely have time for each other, and when we do manage to find time, it often includes work."

"Like the party?"

"Yeah, like the party," she took a deep breath to calm her nerves. "It's easier when it feels like there's an end in sight. Like we're working toward something, but whenever we get close, it feels like someone moves the goalpost."

Thorne nodded. "I wish I didn't understand, but I do. This is why my wife and I divorced."

"You're right; you're not a very good counselor," Grace smiled.

"I'm not telling you that to make you feel bad, silly. I'm pointing it out so you can learn from my mistakes. Unfortunately, we have to work. We also have to do chores, run errands, and in some cases, take care of sick or elderly relatives. But, we don't have to do those things at the exclusion of everything else. Figure out what's important to you, set goals, and let everything else go. If one of your goals is more time with Cole, see what you can do to make it happen."

"I don't want to let anyone down."

"That's part of your control problem. You're trying to control the way everyone feels about you, but you're trying so hard to please everyone else; you're doing it at the expense of your own happiness."

Grace spent some time wiping her eyes and thinking about what he said. His lunch was almost over; she needed to go. "They were wrong about you," she said as she got up and gathered her things.

"Who was?"

"Everyone. Thank you, Thorne." She left before he could respond, more convinced than ever that people were worthy of second chances.

Ten

-Days till 4th of July-

Saturday morning, Grace found herself alone at the hotel, attempting to do some prep work for the party that night while the plumbers, true to their word of working long hours daily, worked on the plumbing. Unfortunately, with the plumbers came an inordinate amount of noise that set her already fragile nerves on edge and made her head hurt. What she had hoped would be a time of reflection had become a time of torture. Which, when she thought about it, could be considered a sign she was not doing what she should be doing.

Thorne had given her a lot to think about the previous day. She was upset her life felt out of control, yet she continued to allow herself to be dragged around by the whims of others. The hotel was a prime example of something she didn't want to do, yet, here she was now, killing herself due to decisions she had not been allowed to help make. Well, that wasn't entirely true. She had protested vehemently but had ultimately been ignored. Which, in her opinion, was worse than having never been consulted at all.

But, as she said to Grant, they were in it now, part of the money she received from Dot's settlement going toward the purchase and renovation of the hotel. Whether she liked it or not, her future was directly tied to this place. Why she had ever agreed to that, well, she knew why she agreed to it. Because, no matter how strongly she felt, she couldn't say the word no.

It was good for her to assess her life. Hopefully, it would help her learn from her mistakes and make better choices in the future. However, dwelling too long on the negative often bought a one-way ticket to pity town. Which, at this point in time, she could not afford.

"Hey," Rebekah called out over the noise of the plumbers.

Startled, Grace spun around, tripped over the paint bucket, and landed on the bed, sending up a cloud of dust that rained down on her paint-splattered face and hair. "Um, hi," she said once she'd caught her breath.

"Are you okay?" Rebekah asked from the doorway.

She had gone still as a statue, her face expressionless as she stared at a wall in the opposite corner of the room. "You're trying not to laugh, aren't you?" Grace asked sarcastically.

"Of course not," Rebekah choked out. Unable to contain her laughter any longer, she backed out of the room and laughed so hard that tears streamed down her face.

"I am not amused," Grace called out from her place on the bed.

That appeared to only make her laugh harder. Some people, Grace thought to herself. She was tempted to stay there, but the dust had gotten in her throat and caused her to erupt in a fit of coughing.

"Here," Rebekah appeared again, this time with a bottle of water.

"Thanks," she took the bottle and downed half in one gulp. "Too bad the bathrooms don't work yet. It would be nice to wash my face."

Rebekah looked in her purse, which Grace was starting to suspect was actually a bag of holding, and pulled out a package of face wipes. "Try these," she said, handing her the package."

"You really do have everything in there, don't you?"

"I used to be a travel blogger, remember?" she shrugged.

"Guess that makes sense. I rarely stray too far from the house, so my purse holds little more than my wallet and keys."

"There's something to be said for having a home you wish to stay close to," she mused.

"Yeah, must have been nice to travel the world, though."

"There are pros and cons to everything," she replied wisely. "Anyway, what's on the agenda for the day?"

Rebekah's abrupt change of topic reminded Grace that, for her, travel had been a means of escape, not something she'd done for fun. "It's interesting," she thought out loud. "How easy it is to take something others envy for granted."

"What do you mean?"

"Nothing," Grace shook her head. "My plan for the day is to do as much cut-in work on these walls as possible so when people show up for the party tonight, all they have to do is roll paint on. It should make things go faster and hopefully help us avoid extra work."

"Isn't the cut-in work the worst part of painting?"

"Yes, it's also the hardest. Which is why I'm doing it. That way, if none of our guests have painting skills, they can still help without creating a mess."

"Sounds good. What can I do to help?"

"You can pick up a brush if you feel confident in your painting ability. If not, it would be really helpful if you could take care of the food and drinks for tonight."

"They don't need to be ready for hours."

"Then I guess you have some free time," she tried to smile, but it wouldn't come. Truth is, she was hoping Rebekah would leave her to her thoughts. Yes, she was trying to stay out of pity town, but being constantly surrounded by people was incredibly draining. Just once, it would be nice to be alone. Even if it was in a hotel full of noisy plumbers.

"If you're sure," she said hesitantly.

"I'm sure."

Rebekah left, but not without looking over her shoulder a few times. It was obvious she wasn't sure what to do; her desire for a day off was at war with her desire to be helpful. At that moment, Grace realized she wasn't the only one who needed to heed Thorne's advice.

***

It was embarrassing to admit, but she had napped in one of the beds while the plumbers were on their lunch break. Of course, she had removed the bedding first. And did a thorough inspection for bed bugs. It was still gross, though. Those mattresses were almost as old as her granny!

It was also embarrassing to have lost track of time and missed her chance to go home to shower and change. She was still covered in paint and dust when the guests arrived for the party, and she was pretty sure she didn't smell as good as she would have liked to, either.

"Don't worry about it," Rebekah whispered when she caught her attempting to wash up with a paper towel and water bottle.

"Easy for you to say," Grace whispered back. "You look like you just stepped off the New York Fashion Week runway. Meanwhile, I look like I've been rolling around in Piper's litter box. I don't suppose you have anything in your purse to fix that?"

"Don't make me laugh," Rebekah snorted.

"I don't know what you're talking about," Grace deadpanned. "Ain't no one laughing over here."

Rebekah laughed harder, eventually putting her hand to her side as she bent at her waist. "Seriously, I can't help you when you make me laugh like that," she wiped at her eyes, careful not to ruin her makeup, then began to dig through her purse. "How about this," she said, pulling out a hairband, a stick of deodorant, and a mascara wand.

"It'll do," Grace said, grateful for any bone Rebekah could throw her way.

"Thanks," she said once she was done. She handed back the items, minus the hairband.

"Glad I could help. Are we ready for the party?"

"Hope so, because here they come."

They watched as their friends filed in through the lobby doors, each taking a turn to marvel and exclaim over the details. "I forgot they've never been here before," Grace said to Rebekah.

"In that case, this party should be considered a treat. Who else gets to say they got a personal tour of this old place?"

"Don't forget to remind them of that if they get tired of painting and start complaining," Grace joked. "Oh look, there's Thorne. And he's dressed like he's here to work!"

"I think I like him better like this," Rebekah said out loud. "He seems so much more normal. More approachable."

Unsure how to respond, Grace stayed silent, although she secretly agreed. Thorne could be an imposing man when he wanted to be, but dressed in ratty old clothes, he looked just like everyone else. Unlike everyone else, his eyes lit up when he saw Rebekah.

"Hey gorgeous," he said as he approached her. "I'm feeling slightly under-dressed here."

"Not compared to me, you're not," said Grace. She was about to comment further when Cole walked in, still wearing his work clothes, pieces of hay popping out here and there. Much like Rebekah, she considered Cole to be at his sexiest when he was in his work clothes.

"Hey," he said when he saw her.

"Hey yourself," she replied. Aware they had an audience, she kissed him anyway, too happy to see him to care. "I know it's kind of early for you. Do you need me to help with the chores later?"

"Riley and I already took care of it."

"Oh, okay then. Are you hungry?"

"I am," said Emilio.

Grace noticed he was holding hands with Vanessa, the two of them obviously still going strong. Looking around, it dawned on her that all her friends were paired off. There was a lot of potential wedding business in this room.

She made quick introductions of Riley, Rebekah, and Thorne, then laid out the plan for the evening, modifying it slightly when they insisted on starting the evening off with a tour.

"I bet this place is haunted," Riley joked when they reached the third floor.

"Don't worry, I'll protect you," Thorne said, pulling Rebekah close.

"My hero," she sighed, dramatically placing a hand backward over her forehead.

"And I'll protect you," Cassie teased Conor.

"My...heroine?" he made a show of swooning in her arms.

The rest of the group laughed and took turns joking until a loud noise came from the room at the end of the hall, effectively ending their antics.

"What was that?" asked Katie. She clutched Riley's arm, clearly concerned and possibly even frightened.

The noise sounded again, louder this time, followed by banging, heavy thuds, and furniture moving around. "What on earth," Grace exclaimed. As the hotel's owner, she made a beeline for the room, anxious to see what was causing the commotion.

"Hold on just a sec," Cole grabbed her arm and pulled her to a stop. "We don't know what's in there," he explained when she tried to yank her arm away.

"Yeah, hence the point of me going to look," she snapped.

"Babe, it could be squatters. We need to be careful, okay."

"Or ghosts," said Katie, who was still clinging to Riley.

Grace turned her face so they couldn't see her roll her eyes. As someone who had spent her life living in an old house, she was more than a little accustomed to things that went bump in the night. Things that typically had a rational explanation, such as the house settling or the furnace rattling the old floor grates. Cole was right, though; squatters were also a rational explanation. "What are you proposing?" she finally asked.

"Let Jake and I go in first, just in case. Please," he said when he saw the annoyance on her face.

"Fine," she agreed. "But I'll be right behind you."

"As long as it's waayyyy behind me," he grinned. He kissed the tip of her nose, then motioned for Jake to follow him down the hall.

Eager to see what was inside, Grace followed at a distance, angling herself to see inside once they opened the door.

"On the count of three," said Cole. "One, two, three," they flung open the door and rushed inside, gagging at the smell as soon as it hit.

"What the heck?" said Grace as she rushed in behind them. "Oh my gosh," she took in the large hole in the ceiling, the old insulation strewn about the room, the knocked-over lamps and furniture. "Why does it smell so bad?"

"Because some animal, or likely animals, is using this room as a bathroom," said Thorne, who had come up behind Grace. "Best guess, either an opossum or a raccoon."

"But how did they get in? I thought the roof was supposed to be new?"

"Did anyone check?" asked Jake.

Grace thought back to her conversation with Grant about waiving their right to an inspection. No one had checked to see if the previous owners had done the work they had claimed; they had simply taken them at their word. "Grant is going to be so mad," said Grace.

"I can help you set traps and relocate the little guys," volunteered Thorne. "But you're going to need to block off their entry point asap if you want to avoid further uninvited guests."

"Can we tarp the roof for now?"

Thorne crinkled his nose. "How about you tack up some plywood instead?"

"I can do that," she covered her mouth and nose with the sleeve of her shirt, the smell quickly becoming unbearable. "How about we get out of here?"

They left the room, carefully closing the door so the critters didn't escape. "How about I go back to my office and grab the traps," said Thorne. "The rest of you can get started on the pizza."

"I'll go with you," said Rebekah.

The two of them left together while the rest of them returned to the lobby. "I bet I have a couple of old sheets of plywood," said Cole. "Give me a few minutes, and I'll run home and get them."

"Take some pizza with you," Grace said, wishing she could go with him.

"I'll help him," Riley said as he grabbed a couple of slices handing one to Cole on the way out.

Grace looked around at the rest of the group, only then realizing that Evie and Jake were bearing witness to the horrid state of the hotel they had reserved for family members. Family members who were supposed to stay there in just a week. This party was indeed the worst idea she had ever had. "Pizza?" she tried to smile as she passed the boxes around, but inside, she wanted to curl up and die.

As they separated into groups, Evie approached Grace, guiding her away from the others. "It's okay," she said quietly.

"I'm so sorry," Grace apologized. "I had no idea—"

"No one's blaming you, including me. Everything is going to work out; you'll see."

"How can you be so calm?" asked Grace.

"Because in ten days I'm marrying my best friend. This," she waved her hand around the hotel. "Is nothing more than a fun story to tell our grandkids."

"Jake is lucky to have you."

"As I am to have him," she hugged Grace. "Do what you can; the rest will work itself out."

"Thank you, Evie."

Evie smiled and returned to Jake, who was laughing and talking with Cassie and Conor. She looked around and saw that everyone else was laughing and talking too. Maybe things really would be okay.

Nine

-Days till 4th of July-

Grace was in the kitchen making breakfast when Grant appeared. "Did things get resolved last night?" he asked.

"Temporarily," she replied.

"What does that mean?"

"It means Cole and Riley were able to patch the hole in the roof, but the entire roof is shot and needs to be replaced. And according to Cole, we're not just talking new shingles. They had a hard time finding places to stand that weren't potential death traps."

"I see," he appeared to be considering what she said. "Looks like the previous owners may not have done the structural repairs they claimed to."

"I did warn you I never saw any work being done," Grace replied. "It's starting to make sense why they chose our offer over the others. Especially since we know that Dot's offer was over the asking price."

"You think they purposefully chose ours because of the inspection waiver?"

"I doubt anyone else was stupid enough to do that. The owners probably thought they'd struck gold when they saw our offer."

"They lied," Grant countered. "We could sue them for damages and probably should."

"Did they lie in writing?"

"What do you mean?"

Grace stopped stirring her batter to look at Grant. Wasn't he supposed to be the expert in all things financial? Why was she, someone who had never bought anything significant in her life, the one asking these questions? "Is there anywhere in the paperwork from the hotel sale that explicitly states they did any work on the building, structural or otherwise?"

Grant ran a hand through his now tousled hair and sighed. "I don't know, I'll have to look. In the meantime, I promised Molly I would take her to breakfast and then to a couple of baby shops she wants to go to."

"Let me know what you find out," Grace said, pasting a fake smile on her face. Must be nice to take a whole day off while everyone else works their rear ends off on your project, she grumbled to herself.

"Will do," he said, utterly oblivious to her inner turmoil.

"I don't hate my friends," Grace repeated over and over again once he'd left.

"Which friends?" Rebekah asked as she came into the room. "I hope I'm not on your list." She narrowed her eyes. "You're not still mad I laughed when you tripped and fell yesterday, are you?"

"What? Oh right," the image of her tripping over the paint bucket and landing on the bed, a cloud of dust rain-ing down on her, flashed before her eyes. "No, I'm not mad about that."

"Then what's going on?"

"Just having a moment of weakness, that's all. What are you up to today?" she asked, mainly to change the subject.

"I was about to ask you that."

"Oh, well, I'm supposed to meet Thorne at the hotel after breakfast so he can check the traps he set last night. After that, the football team is scheduled to come by and help me clear out the rooms so the carpet guys can start laying new carpet tomorrow."

"Do you need me for any of that?"

"No," she answered honestly. "The boys are sure to make short work of it since there's like, what, forty of fifty of them? If even half of them show up, I bet we'll be done in no more than a couple of hours."

"Okay," she hesitated as if she wanted to say more.

Grace looked up from the pan she was using to make pancakes and raised her brow. "Everything okay?"

"I'm going out with Thorne today," she said sheepishly.

"Is that all?"

"It's a big deal," she huffed. "He's taking me out for lunch and then for a game of mini-golf."

"What am I missing?" Grace asked, confused.

"You're missing the part where this isn't for show. It's doubtful we'll run into someone from around here."

She shook her head to clear it, wondering if her lack of sleep was finally getting to her. "You're going on a date with a guy you're supposed to be dating," she said slowly."

"Fake dating, remember. Only, this isn't fake."

"He did say he would take you to a couple of nice restaurants," Grace pointed out.

"This is the first date I've gone on with someone who isn't Hunter," she said quietly.

"Oh," she replied. Now things were starting to make sense. "Thorne is a nice guy; I'm sure you'll have a good time."

"What if I don't?"

"Then you don't," she shrugged. "It's just a date, Rebekah, not a marriage contract. It's okay to decide you just want to be friends."

"Okay, you're right. It's just a date. Between friends," she said to herself. She blew out her breath, causing her bangs to fly up.

"Don't forget, this is technically your second date," Grace reminded her.

Rebekah made a face. "Riley doesn't count."

"Why not?"

"Because it was a double date, and Cole paid. He also drove and picked the restaurant, and I spent most of the night talking to you. There were zero expectations on Riley's part and zero awkward moments of silence while we tried to figure out what to talk about."

The pancakes were finally finished, so Grace pulled the last one off the pan and set the plate on the counter in front of Rebekah. "I never had that problem with Cole," she mused. "If anything, I think I may have talked too much, and that's coming from someone without much to say. You should have zero problems with that."

Rebekah picked up a plate and then put it back down. "I'm too nervous to eat," she admitted. "I think I'll just return to my room and focus on finding something to wear."

"If you need to borrow something, you know where my closet is," said Grace.

"Thanks, you're the best."

***

Grace returned home from the hotel exhausted and in a foul mood. She was too tired to make dinner, but it was Sunday, so that meant gas station pizza was the only option for take-out. Since she had spent the last several days eating enough pizza to last a lifetime, she decided to pass and force herself to cook anyway.

When she opened the back door, she was hit with the smell of something delicious, her feet automatically guiding her toward the scent to see what it was. To her surprise, Rebekah was in the kitchen, stirring something that had to have come from heaven itself.

"What are you making?" Grace asked, pinching herself in case she'd fallen asleep at the hotel again and was dreaming. When she felt pain, she relaxed; at least she wasn't going crazy and hallucinating.

"I had this wonderful pasta at lunch, and I'm trying to recreate the sauce," she explained.

"I'd be willing to bet every cent I have what you're making is a hundred times better than what you had earlier."

Rebekah turned and smiled. "That's very sweet of you, but you didn't have the sauce. Since I'm in a good mood, I will decline to take your bet!"

"How did it go with Thorne?" she asked, changing the subject.

"Once I could relax, we had a great time." She narrowed her eyes at Grace. "You did this on purpose, didn't you," Rebekah accused.

"I thought we already established that?" Grace raised her brow.

"I mean, you chose Thorne, specifically."

"We already established that, too. Thorne is the only bachelor in town; who was I supposed to choose, old man Jenkins?"

Rebekah crinkled her nose. "Why do I know that name?"

"No reason," Grace said dismissively. She was not about to admit to her sophisticated friend she had spent more than her fair share of time watching a kids' cartoon.

"Come on, Grace, be honest with me," she pleaded.

Grace let out a dramatic sigh. "Look, it's really not that complicated. You've told me numerous times you want to find someone special. When I first saw you and Thorne together that day in the kitchen, I thought I saw the possibility of something special."

"When he was yelling at me?" she asked incredulously.

"That was admittedly not great, but you forget that he immediately stopped and apologized the second you called him out. Every man makes mistakes; not every man is willing to own up to them."

"I guess that makes sense. There's still something more going on, though. What aren't you telling me?"

"Isn't it enough to want my friend to be happy?"

"I appreciate that, but do you play matchmaker for all your friends?"

"In case you haven't noticed, I have very few friends. Besides that, the answer is yes. I did my best to nudge Emilio and Vanessa together and did the same with Cassie and Conor. I'm a sucker for romance," she said dramatically.

Rebekah stopped to stare at her for a minute, realization dawning on her. "This has to do with Hunter, doesn't it?"

"Why do you think that?" Grace asked nervously.

"Grace?"

That one word almost broke her, the feelings she'd been holding on to for months unleashing like a tidal wave. "The logical part of my brain knows what happened wasn't my fault. The emotional side can't let go of the feeling I did something horrible."

"I don't understand; what could you have done that was horrible?"

"For a long time, I thought you were the bad guy. That Hunter cheated on me with you. That you were the 'other woman.' I hated you for ruining my relationship with him. Then, I realized I had it backward. I was the 'other woman.'"

"You didn't know. Couldn't have known."

"That doesn't make it easier. I was the lucky one. I met Cole and went on to have the best relationship I've ever had in my entire life while you ended up dumped, disowned, and forced to beg your enemy for a roof over your head so you didn't end up on the streets. I owe you, Rebekah."

Surprised by her admission, Rebekah wrapped her arms around Grace's neck and hugged her. "None of that was your fault," she said softly. "Hunter and I both come from messed up families. All of that would have happened whether we met you or not. I'm the one who's lucky you were here to help me pick up the pieces. If anyone owes anyone, it's me who owes you."

"I just want you to be happy," Grace cried. "Is that really so wrong?"

"You have a bit of a heavy-handed way of going about things," Rebekah laughed. "But no, it isn't wrong. Thank you, Grace. It's been a long time since someone cared enough about me to want me to be happy."

"Was I really that wrong about Thorne?"

"No, you weren't wrong about that either."

"Really?" Grace leaned back to look at her, a hopeful expression on her face.

"We're not ready to send out wedding invitations, but we've agreed to give things a chance. For real this time."

"Yay," Grace squealed. "I'm so happy for you!"

"Calm down," Rebekah laughed. "We don't want to jinx things."

"You're right," she said seriously. They fell silent as Rebekah returned to the stove and Grace sat at the bar. "Thank you for making dinner," she said a few minutes later. "I dreaded having to do it after the day I'd had."

"What happened? Did the boys leave you hanging?"

"No, thankfully, although at this point, I wouldn't have been surprised if they had. It was pure chaos," she groaned. "Forty teenage boys showed up, each with their own plan on how things should work. Jason tried his best to get them to cooperate, but now that he's graduated, they no longer believed they should listen to him. Didn't think they needed to listen to me either."

Rebekah looked at her with her mouth open. "I'm afraid to ask what happened next."

"Multiple contests erupted over who could empty their rooms the fastest, each one crazier than the one before," Grace buried her head in her hands at the memory. "Let's just say we need some new furniture."

"I'm so sorry," said Rebekah. "It was my idea to use the high schoolers. I should have known better."

"No, it's not your fault," Grace said dismissively. "I've used them in the past successfully, but that was when Jason was still their quarterback and commanded respect. Now that he's headed to college this fall, the ones left behind are more interested in trying to replace him than listening to him."

"He sounds like a good kid."

"He really is," she agreed. "His parents raised him right."

"What do we do now? We don't have time to track down new furniture."

"We'll just have to take it from the other rooms and worry about replacing the rest of it later. It still needs to be painted, though, or at the very least, thoroughly cleaned. I shudder to think what kinds of things we'll find in the drawers of those nightstands."

"Maybe we should cancel with the kids from the art club," Rebekah mused. "We don't need another incident like today."

"We don't have time for that either. If we're going to have even a prayer of being ready on time, we need all the help we can get. All we can do now is hope they're better behaved than a group of teenage Neanderthals.

Rebekah laughed at her description. "It's too bad you didn't get all that on film; we could have used it to help market the hotel."

"Only if you plan to call it the 'Smash and Dash Hotel' and market to demolition crews and eighties rock bands."

"I think you missed your calling as a stand-up comedienne!"

"It's never too late."

Eight

-Days till 4th of July-

Evie rushed into the dining room and dropped a stack of white, square envelopes in the center of their breakfast table. "Houston, we have a problem," she announced.

"Muffin?" Grace held up a plate of caramel apple muffins. On the outside, she was cool, calm, and collected. On the inside, she was freaking out, sure that Evie was about to tell her someone had got the date wrong on what was obviously a bunch of wedding invitations, and guests would be arriving earlier than planned. Not that she should be surprised; guests always seemed to come early for one reason or another. She had always done her best to accommodate them, but this was one case in which it would be impossible.

"Thanks," Evie said as she selected one and sat down.

"Wait for me," called a voice from the foyer. "I got here as fast as I could," Cassie panted when she appeared in the doorway. She was out of breath as if she'd run a mile to get there.

"Muffin?" Grace held the plate to her as she selected one and sat down.

"How on earth did you get here so fast?" asked Evie. "I just texted you right before I walked in."

"I was already in town to check on the flowers. When I saw your mayday text, I rushed right over."

Grace poured them each a cup of coffee and set it on the table before them. "So what's the emergency?" she asked, hoping to get the nightmare over quickly, like ripping off a bandaid. The quicker you ripped it off, the less it hurt. Right?

"These are the emergency," she picked up the envelopes and handed them to Grace.

"But, these are addressed to your family members," she narrowed her eyes in confusion as she sorted through the pile. "Did you decide to invite them after all?"

"No, hence the emergency."

"Who's Jesse?" Grace held up an envelope addressed to Shelley and Jesse. Shelley was obviously Evie's sister, but she had no idea who the other person was supposed to be.

"Jesse is the name of Shelley's baby," explained Gladys.

Grace put the envelopes down and looked around the room, completely dumbfounded. "Are you telling me Shelley named her baby after her husband's mistress?"

"I hadn't thought about that," Gladys had a thoughtful expression. "But no, Jesse is the name of the baby's father."

"Still," she shook her head and turned to Evie. "If you didn't send these invitations, then who did?"

"Gloria," she growled.

Grace raised her brow. "The woman who vowed to cancel your wedding because your family is, quote-unquote, without morals, invited them against your will?" When

Evie nodded, Grace shook her head again. "Are we in the twilight zone?"

"That's not even the worst part," she said ominously.

"What could be worse than that?"

"They all said yes."

"It's okay," Rebekah said soothingly. "We'll just call them up, explain there's been a mistake, and politely uninvite them."

"Do you have any idea how big of a scandal that will create?" Evie said, horrified. "People understood when I refused to invite them, but to invite them just to uninvite them? People will think I'm cruel. And my family will do their part to make sure everyone knows how horrible I am for doing that to them."

"Then what do we do? This is a lot of envelopes. Even if they all live nearby, that's a lot of extra people to try accommodating at the last minute."

"I don't know what to do," Evie's voice broke on the last syllable, tears streaming down her cheeks. "We should have eloped," she choked out between sobs. "The thought of those people...after what they did to me...I just can't."

Cassie put her arms around Evie's shoulders and held her tight, Evie burying her face in Cassie's shoulder as she cried. It was too much for Grace to bear. "I'll take care of it," she announced.

Eight sets of eyes turned to look at her. "What are you going to do?" asked Rebekah.

"Don't worry about it," she stood up from the table. "Where is Gloria staying?" she asked Evie.

"At the Red Brick Inn in Hope Springs."

Grace nodded, grabbed her purse and keys from the little table by the back door, and marched to her car. For days, she had promised herself she would start using the word 'no.' Well, today was the day she had been waiting for, and she would start with Gloria.

***

The Red Brick Inn was a cute little hotel appropriately named due to, you guessed it, its red brick facade. Grace had never been inside but had always been curious to know what the rooms looked like. Were they your average, typical hotel room? Or was it something special? Looks like she was about to find out.

Spotting Gloria's car, she parked beside it and got out, checking the sign hanging from the rear-view mirror for her room number. It wasn't the safest way to keep track of guests, but if it worked and no one complained, who was she to judge? She might need something like that someday, although she certainly hoped not.

She raised her hand to knock on the door, but it flew open before she could. "Finally," Gloria exclaimed. "Oh," she said disdainfully when she saw it was Grace. "I thought you were room service."

"Wrong hotel," Grace said dryly.

"No thanks to you," she sniffed. "What do you want? If you're here to apologize, you're too late. There's nothing you could say to get me to forgive you."

"You're out of your mind, lady," she shoved her foot in the door when Gloria tried to slam it shut. "You will listen to what I have to say or—"

"Or what?" she challenged.

"Or you will never see your grandkids."

"Are you threatening to harm my grandchildren?"

Grace rolled her eyes. "No, you old cow, I'm talking about Jake and Evie's children. Which don't exist yet. That stunt you just pulled, the one where you sent invitations to Evie's family, is about to cost you your son, daughter-in-law, and future grandchildren. You are banned from the wedding and will be banned from their life for good. Is that what you want?"

"Jake would never."

"You wanna bet? Don't be surprised when the rest of your family disowns you as soon as they find out what you've done. It's your lack of morals they'll discuss over the wedding cake."

Her anger fizzled out; Grace spun on her heel and marched back to her car. "Just so you know, I'll be calling all your relatives as soon as I get home," she called over her shoulder. It was another lie, but hopefully as effective as the first couple.

"Wait!" she shouted just as Grace was about to close the door. "What am I supposed to do?"

Grace stepped back out of the car. "You can start by undoing the damage you did."

"What does that mean?"

"It means you need to go to Evie's family, apologize for overstepping, and officially uninvite them from the wedding."

Gloria raised her hand to her mouth and gasped. "I could never," she exclaimed. "That would be the epitome of rudeness."

"Inviting people to a private wedding without the bride and groom's permission is the 'epitome of rudeness.' Besides, they deserve it, so don't feel too bad about it."

"Family is family. Evie should make amends with hers before starting a new one with my son."

"That's for her to decide, not you. You've got one chance to make things right, Gloria. Whatever consequences you face will be on you if you refuse to take it."

"I feel like you're threatening me again," she sniffed.

"I never threatened you the first time. Just because you don't like the truth doesn't make it a threat. Also, don't be surprised if Jake and Evie sue you for damages. Not only have you caused severe emotional distress, but you're also costing them thousands of dollars in unexpected fees for the guests you invited and are responsible for."

That last part may have been pushing it, but Gloria was a tough nut to crack. If losing out on a relationship with future grandchildren wasn't enough to spur her into action, maybe the thought of financial consequences would. If that didn't work, nothing would.

"I'll take care of it," Gloria said softly. So softly Grace had to strain to hear.

"Promise?"

Gloria nodded, a look of resignation on her face. "If I do this, will I be allowed to attend the wedding?"

"I can't make any promises, but I'll talk to Evie. It doesn't have to be this way, you know?"

"What do you mean?"

"I mean, you don't have to make everyone your enemy. You could choose instead to be the kind of mother and grandmother your family wants to be around. Not the kind they have to shove in a hotel thirty minutes away."

"I'll take that under consideration." Room service chose that moment to arrive, effectively ending their conversation.

With nothing left to say, Grace got back in her car and headed home, hopeful her words had hit their mark. If Gloria chose not to make things right, Grace would track down Evie's family members. Under no circumstances was she going to allow her friend's day to be ruined by a group of spiteful people.

***

Later that night, Evie, Cassie, Jake's sister Megan, her young daughter Violet, and the one family member Evie was still talking to, Mandy, checked in to the b&b. Grace was busy making dinner for everyone while the five of them, plus Rebekah, discussed flower arrangements at the dining room table. Violet, who Grace estimated to be around five, colored quietly while Piper slept curled up in her lap.

Thankfully, the atmosphere had significantly improved as the day wore on; laughter replaced the tears, and excitement replaced the anxiety, at least for the ones at the table. Grace still had a mountain of work, and the clock was ticking.

Just as she pulled the dinner rolls out of the oven, a knock sounded at the front door. "I'll get it," she said to herself. Her guests were too busy exclaiming over pictures in magazines to have noticed.

To her surprise, Gloria was standing on the other side when she opened the door. "What can I do for you?" she asked cautiously.

"I did what you said," she mumbled so quietly Grace could barely hear her.

"I'm sorry, I didn't quite catch that."

Gloria sighed. "I did what you said, okay?"

Grace stepped back to give Gloria room to enter the house. "Evie's inside. Would you like to tell her yourself?"

"I don't know," she hesitated. "I don't want to cause any more problems."

"If you're truly sorry, and want to make amends, now is the perfect time," Grace told her.

"Okay," she took a deep breath and stepped inside, listening for a moment to the voices in the other room. "Megan's here?"

"Yes, Violet too," she motioned for her to follow, then led the way into the dining room. "Evie," she shouted to get her attention. "Someone is here to see you."

Evie looked up, the smile immediately leaving her face when she saw Gloria. "I really don't want any more trouble," she told the woman.

"This won't take long," Gloria told her. "I just came to apologize and to let you know that I personally visited each of your family members and uninvited them from the wedding. I can't promise they won't still try to show up," she continued. "But I made it clear they are no longer welcome. Were never welcome."

"I don't know what to say," said Evie. Tears shined in her eyes. "Thank you."

"You don't have to thank me for doing the right thing. I should have never invited them in the first place. What I did was wrong, and I'm ashamed of myself for doing it."

"Wow, Mom, I'm proud of you," said Megan. "It took a lot of courage to come here and admit that."

"Took a lot of courage to face my family," said Evie.

Gloria nodded. "Well, I don't want to take up any more of your time, so I'll see myself out." she turned to leave when Evie called her back.

"Wait," she said. "We're trying to decide on centerpieces for the tables, but we can't seem to agree. Would you like to help?"

The shock on Gloria's face quickly turned to one of joy. "I would love to," she said. "If you're sure?" she asked hopefully.

"You can sit by me, Grandma," said Violet, patting the chair beside her.

Grace wiped a tear from her eye as she watched Gloria sit next to Violet and hug her. Gone were the animosity and barely concealed hostility from the other day. Gloria had taken her words to heart and decided to choose family. The inn of miracles hadn't lost its touch after all. If only Grace could get one of those miracles to transfer to the hotel.

Seven

-Days till 4th of July-

The morning had started off like any other, sunny and hot. She did her chores at the farm, served breakfast, and then, while everyone else made fun plans for the day, started the list of food she would need for the upcoming weekend. The shopping trip she had planned was so big she required Cole's truck to haul it all home.

"Do you need anything from us before we leave?" asked Evie. She was dressed in a cute summer dress, her bridal week officially began.

"Nope," Grace replied absentmindedly. The list now covered two pages; she only had four hours to complete it. It was going to be a long day.

"What do you have planned for the day?" asked Cassie as she peeked over her shoulder.

"Hm," she looked up to see them all looking at her expectantly. "Oh, uh, let's see. First, I need to go to the warehouse store and shop for food. Then, I'm meeting the art club at the hotel to continue painting the furniture.

Then, I'll be back here to make dinner, then it's back to the hotel to meet Thorne, then back here to—"

"Grace!" Evie held up her hand to get her to stop. "That is way too much, girlfriend."

"I need a nap just from hearing your list," joked Cassie.

"What's this about painting furniture?" asked Megan.

"The furniture at the hotel is old and dated, so we're trying to give it a bit of a makeover," Grace explained.

"I love painting furniture," Megan replied enthusiastically. "It's one of my favorite hobbies. Do you need some help?"

Boy, did she, Grace thought. "You guys already have plans," Grace answered without answering. She desperately wanted to say yes, but Evie had been looking forward to spending time with her friends before the wedding, and she would feel terrible if she ruined that for her.

"Our plans can be changed," said Evie. "Our painting party the other night was fun; this should be too!"

Had Evie always been an eternal optimist? Grace wasn't sure. What she was sure about was that Evie was incredibly kind and was more likely agreeing to be helpful than because she actually wanted to spend her afternoon painting old furniture. "I don't know, guys; the art club has made some decent progress; I bet we can handle it."

"We'll meet you at the hotel around one," Evie stated firmly. "No arguments," she said when Grace opened her mouth. "Do you need help with the shopping?"

Grace shook her head. "Cole is going with me."

Evie eyed her suspiciously, then nodded. "See you later then."

"Have fun!" Grace called out cheerfully. Inside she groaned. She was not doing as good of a job hiding her feelings as she thought. The image of a frazzled, anxiety-ridden b&b hostess was not the look she was going for. She must do better. She would do better.

Thorne's words came back to her, causing her to stop and take a deep breath. It's okay, she repeated to herself. I'm doing the best I can. If that's not good enough, too bad, I can't do any more than I already am.

The mini panic attack passed, and she immediately felt better. "I can do this," she said out loud. Her phone dinged, and she looked to see Cole had texted he was outside. Excited to see him, she grabbed her purse and ran out to greet him, practically pole-vaulting into his truck in her haste.

"Goodness," he laughed. "Nice to see you too," he drawled.

"It feels like it's been forever," she whispered into his neck.

"It's only been a couple of hours, darlin'."

"Sounds like I was right," she agreed. "It has been forever.

Cole hugged her tight as he chuckled against the side of her head. "At least we have some time together now," he leaned her back and kissed her, eager to show how glad he was to see her.

"I have to be at the hotel by one," she informed him.

"Guess we better hurry then," he said after checking his watch.

"With the time it takes to get there and back, we only have two hours to shop," she said.

"If we take two hours, you won't have time to put everything up when you get back," he replied as he pulled away from the curb and up to the stop sign.

Grace sighed and laid her head on his shoulder. "I forgot about that."

"It won't be as fun, but we can divide your list, each taking half. It shouldn't take long if we tackle our halves separately."

"That defeats the purpose of us shopping together," she said irritably. "This was supposed to be a way for us to spend time together."

"What will happen if you aren't at the hotel by one?"

What would happen, indeed? "If I'm not there to open the door, the kind people who agreed to donate their time and skill to help me out won't be able to do the job they agreed to do," she sighed for the one-millionth time that morning.

"I might be able to squeeze in some time together tonight?" he raised his brow in question.

"I'm supposed to meet Thorne after dinner to check the traps. We've only caught one possum so far, and he's convinced there's at least one more hiding out there."

"After?"

"Your place or mine?"

"Mine," he said quickly. "No offense, but I'd rather not run into your guests."

"You afraid of a group of women?" she teased.

"I'm afraid of getting stuck talking to them when I'd rather be alone with you."

"Your place it is."

***

She met Thorne at the hotel at seven o'clock to check the traps. Since it was so hot, she had checked them every few hours she was there, just in case, but there was still no sign of the missing critter. She had informed Thorne of her findings, or lack thereof, but he had insisted on coming by anyway. According to him, it was strange to have gone days without catching the little guy, especially since they'd cut off his escape route. Grace was concerned that meant they hadn't cut it off, but Thorne claimed the trap could be faulty, hence his trip to check.

Honestly, Grace had been grateful for an excuse to leave the house. It had been a long day, and as much as she liked everyone, she was exhausted and in no mood for fun and games. She really craved an evening cuddling on the couch with Cole in front of the fireplace like they used to. Minus the fire, of course. All she needed to do was get through her appointment with Thorne.

"Hey," she greeted him when she exited her car. He had been waiting for her when she pulled up, clearly interested in getting out of there quickly as well.

"Hey," he replied. "This shouldn't take long."

Once inside, they made a beeline for the stairs, Thorne taking them two at a time as Grace struggled to catch up. When they reached the third floor, they went straight to the room at the end of the hall. "Have you seen any signs the possum's still around?" he asked.

Grace shook her head. "As far as I can tell, there haven't been any new bathroom activities. He hasn't drank any of the water I sat out either."

"This is so strange," he said.

They opened the door, went inside, and looked around. As Thorne checked the trap, Grace watched from the doorway. "What do you think?" she asked when he set it back down.

"No sign that it's broken or malfunctioning. At this point, it might be safe to assume I was wrong and there was only one uninvited guest."

She looked around the room at the mess. "One possum did all of this?" she swept her hand across the room.

"It's unlikely, but I don't know," he threw up his hands. "Maybe the other one escaped before Cole and Riley closed the hole. "For now, keep checking the traps; maybe check the other rooms a time or two, just in case."

"Will do," she said.

"How are things going," he asked as they returned downstairs.

They moved at a slower pace; the need to rush was no longer necessary. "Okay," she said. It was already obvious where this was going, so she decided to head him off. "I was thinking about our conversation the other day," she said slowly. "You said you and your wife divorced due to busy schedules; is that right?"

"Yes," he nodded. "I was working somewhere between sixty to eighty hours a week on a steady basis."

"Wow," Grace whistled. "I thought only emergency room doctors had that kind of schedule?"

"That is fairly typical for them and untypical for us. But, I did an internship at an exotic animal clinic in the rich part of the city before I graduated. I thought I'd won the lottery when they offered me a full-time position. I was one of the highest-paid veterinarians of my graduating class. I didn't realize the clinic had a reputation for overworking their new doctors, giving them all the overnight and weekend shifts the other doctors no longer wanted to work."

"Why did you stay?"

"I mistakenly believed that if I put in the time, paid my dues, so to speak, I would work my way up the ladder and eventually become one of the experienced doctors with the good shifts and benefits."

"But it didn't happen?"

"Not in the time I was there. I spent five years working for that place, and all I have to show for it is an ex-wife who hates me."

Grace put her hand on his arm. "I'm so sorry," she said compassionately.

"Thank you," he grabbed her hand and squeezed. "In the end, everything turned out okay."

"I don't understand; there was a rumor that you were forced to come here due to some kind of scandal. Did the last vet fire you or something?"

"There are those rumors again," he shook his head. "I don't know how or why that started, but it couldn't be further from the truth. I came here because I wanted a fresh start and, more importantly, a job where I could work normal hours. I needed to slow down, and a job in a small, rural town seemed like a great place to do it."

"Minus the overnight house calls," she teased.

"There has been a surprising lack of those," he replied. "I expected a lot more, but these old farmers have been around birthing animals so long, they only need me when something goes horribly wrong, which, thankfully, isn't often."

They reached their cars and pulled out their keys. "I hope you took my advice to heart," he said gently. "Burning the candle at both ends rarely leads to anything but heartache."

"I'm trying to," she told him. "I just need to get through the wedding. After that, I should be able to slow down."

"After that, something else will come up; it always does. If you want change, you will have to make it happen. Trust me on that."

He waved goodbye and got in his car, leaving her alone on the sidewalk. Wasn't that the same thing she had told herself the other day? What changes could she make? She could refuse to do any more work on the hotel, but all that would do is delay their opening, and they couldn't afford that. At the very least, she could refuse any more events at the b&b until at least Halloween. That would give them almost three solid months without guests to worry about.

Convinced she had found at least part of a solution, she got in her car. Cole was waiting, and for once, they could spend the whole night together without interruptions. What more could she ask for?

Six

-Days till 4th of July-

Pressed for time, Grace swung through Addie's on the way back from the ranch to pick up a dozen of her breakfast specials. Since she had called ahead, she could quickly get in and out with her order. Back home, she placed the containers in the oven to stay warm and then got ready.

"Where you headed off to?" asked Rebekah with a yawn. She was tired; her usually styled hair was thrown on top of her head in a bun, her clothes wrinkled and unmatching.

"To the hotel," Grace mumbled through the keys in her mouth. She juggled multiple boxes, trying not to trip over the cat weaving through her legs.

"Isn't it a little early for that?" she yawned again, clearly needing at least another hour or two of sleep. Or, at the very least, a strong cup of coffee.

"Could you get the cat, please?" she said as she stumbled, a couple of the boxes falling to the floor.

"Sorry," Rebekah rushed forward and grabbed Piper, snuggling her against her chest. "If you give me a minute, I can help load those in your car."

"I don't have a minute. The delivery truck is scheduled to arrive at eight o'clock. Breakfast is in the oven. I'll see you later." She rushed out the door, figuring she would return for the rest of the boxes later.

Now that the carpet guys had finished, Grace could assemble the rooms. Since the furniture company had agreed to deliver the mattresses today, she had the art club prioritize the bed frames, which were now freshly painted and ready to go. Jason and his buddies, the well-behaved ones, had agreed to help her set up the beds, which to her, felt like a miracle. She would miss him when he left for school in a couple of months

The delivery truck pulled into the lot just as she parked her car, proof that she hadn't been lying when she said she didn't have a minute. The boys were right behind, amped up and ready to work. She caught herself wishing for their youth and energy, then realized she was only seven years older than them. When had she become elderly in her own mind? Honestly, this business felt like it had aged her at least two decades in the last six months. She would end up in a nursing home by the end of the year at the rate she was going. At least she'd have Granny and Gladys to keep her company.

Twenty sets of mattresses later, Grace was ready to say goodbye to the movers when they reminded her they also had twenty mini-fridges to drop off. With a deep sigh, she called the boys back out and began to unload. The mini-fridges had been her idea, a simple way to provide drinks and snacks to the guests since meals had become such a problem. But that was before she understood the electrical wiring was an issue. Were mini-fridges a thing in the sixties? Could this old wiring handle twenty of them running at the same time? Did she really want to find out the hard way?

"Breakfast is here," came a voice from the foyer.

Grace hurried out of the room she was in to meet Jenny. "Thanks," she said gratefully. "These guys have been working hard and are probably starving by now."

Jenny laughed. "They're always starving; it comes with the territory."

"She's not wrong," said Jason as he grabbed a breakfast sandwich.

The other guys grabbed a sandwich and followed him into the dining room. "Do you need anything else?" asked Jenny.

"We don't seem to be moving as fast as I thought. Any chance we could get lunch too?"

"It's barbecue sandwich day," Jenny replied.

"Perfect," her eyes lit up at the mention of Addie's famous sandwiches.

"Two each?" she asked, counting the number of guys that had shown up to help.

"Plus another dozen or so for the b&b."

"Sounds good," she smiled at Grace. "Don't worry; I'll get them dropped off in time. At both places."

"You're a lifesaver," she gave the woman a generous tip and walked her outside.

"Just remember that the next time you decide to play matchmaker!"

"I will make sure to send the next eligible bachelor I stumble upon your way," Grace joked.

"I'm gonna hold you to that. Be back in a few hours."

Grace joined the rest of the group in the dining room, careful to grab a sandwich before they were all gone. "If you're worried about the electrical, you should have John come by and check things out. He should be able to tell you if the wiring can handle the load," said Jason.

"You mean John Langford?" she asked, naming the local electrician. "I'm too scared he'll tell me the answer is no."

"Probably be better to find that out before, don't you think? The last thing you want is a fire to break out with over forty people trapped in the building."

"You're right," Grace sighed. "I'm out of time and backup plans, though. What should I do if he tells me we aren't safe to operate?"

"Make reservations at hotels in neighboring towns and then rent a bus," said Kyle.

That was such a simple and easy solution; she wished she had thought of it before. They wouldn't have made any money on the hotel stays, but it would have made more sense than killing themselves or, more specifically, her. At least now, she would have a backup plan. "I'll call John," she said, pulling out her phone. If she was lucky, he could meet her while she was there with the guys.

***

Late afternoon found Grace back at the house, hard at work making casseroles. She and the boys had finished assembling the beds and moving the furniture into place right before lunch. The electrician had shown up, declared the hotel a disaster waiting to happen, but said he could do enough to get them safely through the weekend. The mini-fridges had not been the problem; the air conditioners had been. It would cost them, of course, but nowhere near what it would cost if the place caught fire.

Grant was unhappy with the additional fees, but Grace didn't care; it needed to be done. Besides, she wasn't the one who decided to rent a bunch of rooms to guests in freaking July. In a dilapidated, old hotel to boot!

"Something sure smells good," said Rebekah as she entered the kitchen.

"Thanks, I'm making enchiladas. Next up is lasagna, then a chicken parmesan, and then a chicken pot pie."

"All that for dinner tonight?" she asked in surprise.

"No, tonight I'm grilling kebabs. This is for the upcoming weekend."

"Oh, okay. Do you need any help?"

"In about twenty minutes, I need to run over to Gladys's and take some pans out of the oven. If you've got time?"

"Sure," she said as her phone rang. "I need to get this," she said when she saw who it was.

As Rebekah walked out the back door, someone knocked on the front. Grace wiped her hands and went to the door, hoping whoever it was wouldn't take long. When she opened the door, she got the surprise of her life. "What are you doing here?" she asked Shelley.

"What do you think? I'm here to see my sister." She held a baby in one arm and a suitcase in the other.

"She isn't here," Grace replied, nervous about what this woman had in mind.

"Don't lie to me; her car is right over there," she gestured to the driveway on the side of the house.

Already fed up with Shelley's attitude, Grace contemplated shutting the door in her face. "Her car may be here, but she isn't. Look, Shelley, I don't have time for this. You aren't welcome here for obvious reasons, so please leave."

"Evie is my sister," she pouted. "I should be her maid of honor, not Cassie. I'm here to make things right," she held up her suitcase as she gestured toward it.

Realization dawned on Grace as she opened her mouth wide in horror. "You can't seriously expect your sister to make you her maid of honor after what you did to her?"

Shelley rolled her eyes. "That doesn't count. Besides, she should consider it a favor after what Greg did to me. She should be thanking me," Shelley huffed.

"I'm pretty sure she doesn't see it that way," Grace said dryly. "Anyway, I'll give Evie your message when she returns." Grace moved to shut the door.

"Wait!" she exclaimed. "I'll just wait inside, and then I can give her the message myself."

Grace used all five foot two, one hundred and twenty pounds of herself to block Shelley's entrance. "I'm sorry, but now is not a good time. I'll have Evie call you later."

"I have nowhere else to go," she whined.

"I thought you were living with your parents?"

"Are you crazy? I can't live with them while Greg lives with his mistress and their baby. It's too embarrassing."

"Weren't you living with them before you married Greg?"

"Yeah, but it was different then. No one batted an eye at a single woman still living at home. I'm about to be divorced with a child."

"I don't see how that's my problem," Grace told her. "This is a b&b, not an apartment complex. Even if Evie is willing to let you stay, which I highly doubt, you will still need a place to live come Tuesday. Best to get that sorted now."

Fat teardrops began to slide down her cheeks. She put down her suitcase and held the baby out for Grace to see. "Have you no heart?" she asked in a pitiful voice. "Are you really going to put a mother and her baby out on the street?"

This little pity party had gone on long enough. "Go home, Shelley," she said in a tone that brokered no argument; without a second thought, she went inside, locking the door behind her.

"I was just about to go to Gladys's," said Rebekah when they met in the dining room. "Am I too late?"

Grace checked her watch. "No, but go the back way. You won't believe this, but Shelley's out front, and I wouldn't be surprised if she refuses to leave until she's talked to Evie."

"You're kidding!"

"I wish I was."

"What does she want?"

"To stay here with Evie and take over maid-of-honor duties. Although, I guess it would be matron-of-honor duties? Or does it count if she's about to get divorced?" Grace waved a hand dismissively. "Never mind, I don't care enough to know."

Rebekah laughed. "I'll do my best to avoid her. Be back in a few minutes."

It was easier than she thought it would be to continue as if there wasn't a seriously deluded and entitled woman on her front porch. Some part of her felt bad for the baby, but his mother was responsible for caring for him, not Grace. If she was willing to wait outside in the heat, that was on her. Grace just hoped the baby didn't pay for his mother's mistakes. Maybe she should try to find out who this Jesse person was and give him a call.

"How are things going?" asked Gladys. She was carrying a cup in each hand, which would typically not be a big deal, but for someone with a bad hip, it could prove catastrophic if she needed to suddenly reach out to grab something.

"Let me help you," Grace hurried over to Gladys and removed the cups. "If you needed a drink, you could have called. I would have brought you one.

"Nonsense," she said. "This old bag-o-bones can handle getting some water once in a while."

That was debatable, but Grace didn't want to upset her, so she let it go. "How about you sit at the breakfast bar and talk to me for a minute while I get you those drinks?"

Gladys gave her the side-eye, but she did as asked. "Is there something you want to talk about?"

"Who's Jesse?"

"As in, the father of Shelley's baby?"

Grace nodded, then proceeded to fill the cups with ice. "Is he local?"

"He works at Garrison's Garage; why do you ask?"

"Because Shelley is outside on the front porch refusing to leave. It's so hot out there I thought someone should check on the baby. Jesse seemed the least offensive of the options."

"I'll call him," Gladys got up to get her phone. When she came back, she informed Grace that Jesse was on his way.

"Why isn't Shelley moving in with him?" asked Grace. "It's not like she's getting back together with Greg."

"I guess Shelley's family doesn't think he's good enough."

"He was good enough to get her knocked up," Grace pointed out.

"In secret, dear. All that happened in secret."

"Not anymore."

A commotion on the front porch drew their attention. Grace and Gladys exchanged a look, then went to investigate. Outside, multiple people were milling about in varying degrees of agitation.

"You're crazy," said Cassie. She was nose to nose with Shelley; the only thing separating them was the baby.

"I'M HER SISTER," Shelley shouted, her raised voice waking the baby in her arms.

"Give him to me," Jesse said sternly. He pushed his way in between the women and took the crying baby. "If this is how you're going to act, I'm taking the baby and raising him by myself," he informed a visibly distressed Shelley.

"You can't do that," she cried. "My family will never let you take him from me."

"Your family will have no choice once I take you to court," he replied.

"Guys!" said Gladys, loud enough to be heard over the noise. "That's enough of this. Jesse, please take Shelley and the baby home," she turned to Shelley. "Young lady, if you know what's good for you, you will go with that man and do your best to work with him to raise your son. Your family's influence will only get you so far."

"This isn't fair," she whined.

"You have only yourself to blame. You're a mother now; it's time for you to take responsibility for your actions."

"Let's go," said Jesse.

He was so upset, Grace wasn't sure who she felt sorrier for, him or the baby. Thankfully, Shelley followed him, though the look on her face showed this was far from over. "Let's go inside," Grace said to everyone.

The ladies followed, grumbling among themselves over the incident. "I'm sorry about that," Grace said to Evie once they were inside. "She refused to leave until you came back."

"It's okay; I should have expected something like this," she shook her head. "I should have eloped."

Five

-Days till 4th of July-

"Oh good, you're here," Grace said when she entered the dining room and found Rebekah seated at the table. "In your opinion, how important would it be to have mirrors in the hotel rooms?"

"On a scale from one to ten?"

"Sure," Grace nodded.

"Ten. The guests are coming for a wedding and will want to avoid cramming into the bathroom together to get ready. If they have a mirror, they can at least do their hair and make-up in their rooms."

"That's what I was afraid you would say," Grace groaned.

"Forgot about the mirrors?" she asked compassionately.

"Yeah, forgot about the mirrors. Guess I better make another trip to the furniture store." She sounded defeated, even to herself. There was no time for mistakes, yet she kept making them anyway.

"Check at some of the home décor stores first. They'll likely be cheaper and easier to purchase. If we can go now, I can go with you and help you pick them out."

Grace looked at her watch and winced. "I need to call Cole and see if I can borrow his truck. There's no way we'll cram twenty large mirrors in the back of the Corolla."

"While you do that, I'll get ready to go. Be back in five."

One quick call to Cole later, and they were in business. While he was not able to go, Riley was. Which might lead to a bit of awkwardness, but at this point, she couldn't afford to care. Some day soon, she would need to invest in a truck. She couldn't keep bothering Cole whenever she needed to haul stuff around. Which, these days, was often.

"Ready to go?" Rebekah asked.

"Yeah, Riley should be here any minute."

"Riley?"

"Cole was too busy, so he volunteered Riley. I hope that isn't a problem?"

"Not for me," she shrugged.

The trip to the store was reminiscent of the one she took to the warehouse a few days before, only this time, Rebekah was the one in the middle seat. It would have been comical if Katie hadn't been outside town hall when they passed by on their way out. Judging by her look, she was unhappy to see her perceived competition sitting next to her boyfriend. It was clear to everyone but her that Riley and Rebekah were just friends. Eventually, she would need to accept that or risk losing him over her jealousy.

"Where to first, ladies?" he asked, seemingly oblivious to the trouble coming his way. He had happily waved to Katie as he passed by and either missed the look on her face or intentionally ignored it.

"I think Woodlands would be a good place to start," said Rebekah.

"We don't have a store named Woodlands," said Grace.

"Obviously, Winterwood doesn't, but surely you have one in the city."

"Nope, not that I'm aware of," said Grace.

Rebekah pulled out her phone and opened the map. After a few minutes of typing, she put it back in her purse and sighed. "Okay, no Woodlands. How about that home store? Is it any good?"

"I'm no expert, but it seemed nice enough when we went there for Christmas decorations."

A look difficult to interpret crossed Rebekah's face. Grace wasn't sure, but the look likely had something to do with Hunter. Would that man never cease to be a source of pain and consternation? "Let's try there then," she finally said.

Three stores, two coffee shops, and one stop for lunch later, they had the mirrors they needed. They were all different, but they were large, so hopefully, that would be good enough. They were just about to head out of town when Grace had a thought. "What about televisions?" she asked them.

"What about them?" asked Riley.

"The hotel doesn't have any. Do you think that'll be a problem?"

The look on Riley's face was all the answer she needed. "Is there room for twenty T.V.s in the back of the truck?" she asked him.

Riley turned in his seat to survey the back of his truck. "If we do a little rearranging, I think we can manage."

"Where should we go to get them?" she asked out loud.

"Wait a minute," Rebekah held up her hand. "Unless the hotel has cable, satellite, or internet, these T.V.s will be nothing more than paperweights."

Grace rolled her eyes. It was always one thing after another with this hotel. "On a scale of one to ten, how important do you think it is to have a T.V. in the rooms?" she asked them.

"Ten," they replied in unison.

"I don't watch a lot of T.V.," he said. "But if I checked into a hotel and it didn't have one, I'd be pretty disappointed."

"I agree," said Rebekah. "I doubt there's a single hotel in America that doesn't have them in every room. It's as American as apple pie."

"Well, shoot, guys. What am I supposed to do now?"

"Let's go to one of those big box stores and buy the cheapest ones we can find. They may not last forever, but at least they'll get you through the weekend," said Riley.

"And the cable?"

"Call one of those satellite companies on the way to the store. I'm sure they would be happy to help you out for a job this big," said Rebekah.

"Okay, let's do it." Grace sighed again as she pulled out her phone. To her knowledge, this was not a problem at the b&b. At least, no one had ever complained. Maybe people had been upset and just never said anything. She should ask her former guests for their feedback. Conor, Emilio, Vanessa, and Rebekah were all still around. She could also ask her current guests.

When she first opened the b&b, it was all about an old-fashioned Christmas experience. At no point did that scream television to her. But it wasn't about her; it was about her guests. If she planned to stay in the hospitality sector and be successful, she would need to remember that.

***

When they finally returned to the b&b, it was to a house in chaos. Evie, Gladys, Granny, and the rest of the girls sat at the dining room table; Evie sobbed in her arms as the rest looked on in despair.

"What happened?" asked Grace. She was sure someone had died and immediately went through the list of people she knew. "Is it Jake?" she asked, her eyes widening in horror.

"No," Cassie reassured her. "Jake's fine. Everyone is fine."

"Then why is she crying?"

"Shelley has spent the day telling everyone who will listen that her sister threw her and her baby out on the street. She's accused Evie of being jealous of her and taking it out on her nephew."

Grace put her arm on Evie's shoulder. "Surely no one believes this," she looked at Gladys questioningly.

Gladys shrugged her shoulders. "There's a certain crowd who believe family trumps everything."

"Did they believe that when Shelley ran off with Evie's fiance?"

"Hypocrites rarely acknowledge their own hypocrisy," she replied.

"I think I know how to solve this," Grace told the group. "I'll be back in a little bit."

It was the time of day between lunch and dinner, but Grace knew the usual suspects could still be found at the diner. They could always be found at the diner, as they had nothing better to do than hang out, drink coffee, and gossip. Addie tolerated it because their money was good, and chasing them out would hurt her more than it would them. They weren't malicious; they were just busybodies. But for once, Grace planned to use that to her advantage.

"Hey guys," she waved to the group when she entered the diner, then proceeded to move to the counter and study a menu. She knew it was only a matter of time before they called her over.

"Grace," Gary, the group's unofficial spokesman, called out. "Come sit with us a spell."

Smiling to herself, she turned to oblige. "What can I do for you?" she asked as she sat beside Marge.

"What's going on out at the b&b? We heard you threw Shelley out on the street?"

Gladys had not mentioned that part. She widened her eyes and shook her head, a look of horror on her face. "Oh no, I would never!" she exclaimed. "Shelley came by yesterday but left with Jesse and the baby."

"Then why is she telling people that you and Evie turned her away?"

Grace leaned in close and said in a stage whisper. "Shelley told me she couldn't stay with her parents anymore. I think it has something to do with Jesse...." she made a face and looked away, hopeful they would get her meaning.

Marge gasped. "You don't mean because he's poor?"

She refused to look in their direction. "You know I'm not one to gossip...."

"Of course not, dear," Marge patted her hand. "You know," she leaned in to whisper just as Grace had. "It wouldn't surprise me if that's true. I bet they had no problem with Greg's situation because his family comes from money. I bet they're furious their first grandchild came from a mechanic. Probably think it will soil their family line."

"They are old money," said Gary. "At least in these parts," he let out a bark of laughter. "If they tried to go somewhere where real old money lived, they'd be laughed all the way back home."

"If you ask me," Grace said, trying to keep them on topic. "Jesse is a step up from Greg. He has a full-time job, is dependable, and doesn't have a reputation for being a womanizer. I mean, Greg did just have a baby with another woman."

"Shelley wasn't exactly innocent," Marge reminded them.

"No," Grace sighed dramatically. "But I'm hopeful motherhood will change her. They deserve a chance to be a real family, right?"

Gary and Marge nodded enthusiastically. "That poor baby," Marge clucked.

Grace wasn't sure which 'baby' she was referring to, but it seemed her work here was done. She felt a little slimy, but sometimes it was necessary to fight fire with fire. Jake's family would arrive in just two days. She couldn't let them roam around town hearing slanderous gossip about Evie. Since they didn't know her, they wouldn't know what to believe. Shelley's attempts to ruin Evie's life have gone unchecked long enough.

"I just hope they're able to work things out," Grace said. "You know how that family is about appearances. They'll say and do anything to make themselves look good." Her work done, she got up to leave. "I have to get back to the b&b," she told them. "It was nice talking to you guys!"

"Nice talking to you, too," said Marge.

Not wanting to look suspicious, Grace went to the counter and ordered one of Addie's premade coconut pies to go. Addie wrapped up the pie, gave her a knowing wink, then said her goodbyes, Grace giving a little wave to the group on her way out.

Back home, she addressed the group still seated at the table. "Everything should be okay now," she informed them.

"Why, what happened?" Evie asked, raising her head to look at Grace.

"In a way, I told the truth."

"What do you mean, 'in a way'?" asked Gladys.

"In mean, I told it in a way that people will want to gossip about," Grace demurred.

"Grace!" Granny admonished. "You know better than to spread rumors."

"As I said, it was the truth. Regardless, someone had to say something. If I didn't, people might actually believe the garbage coming out of Shelley's mouth."

Grace set the pie on the table and slid it into the middle. "Anyway, here's a pie. I need to go to the hotel, so consider this your afternoon snack."

Rebekah followed her to the door. "Are you okay," she asked softly, so no one could overhear.

"I'll be fine."

"You don't seem fine."

"I'm tired of this," she whispered as tears stung the back of her eyes. "All this drama and nonsense is wearing me down. I miss when life was simpler."

"When was that?"

"When was what?"

"When was life simpler?"

She thought about it for a minute. "Before Christmas, I think. Before Granny got sick, to be more precise."

"Was it simpler, or was it empty?"

"What do you mean?"

"I mean, before all this' drama and nonsense,' you were a lonely woman with no friends, no job, and no Cole. Now, you have all those things. Aren't they worth a little pain and suffering?" When Grace hesitated to answer, Rebekah continued. "Because they're worth it to me."

Grace looked up at her in her surprise. She opened her mouth to reply, but Rebekah cut her off. "Before I came here, I had a fiance who didn't want to marry me, friends who only liked me because of my family's wealth and social status, no job, and no purpose. Thanks to you, I now have all those things. Well, minus the fiance part. Although, someday, I might even have that too. You've helped a lot of people. Don't give up just because things seem hard."

"Thanks," Grace replied automatically, trying to take it all in. "It wasn't that long ago you were mad at me over the 'fiance' part," she reminded her.

"I was wrong," she sniffed. "I don't say that often, so you should appreciate it."

Grace laughed at the 'old Rebekah.' "I do appreciate it," she said honestly. "And you're right; I'll do my best to change my perspective."

"That's all anyone can ask," she replied.

Four

-Days till 4th of July-

The sound of screams woke Grace from a dead sleep. Confused, she looked at her alarm clock to see it was three in the morning. Was the screaming real? Or was it part of a dream? Seconds later, she had an answer.

After throwing on a bathrobe, she rushed into the hall where several women had congregated. "What's going on?" she asked the group.

"There's a possum in my room," said Evie. She was standing with her back to her bedroom door, holding the doorknob tight as if to keep it closed.

"I don't think possums can open doors," said Grace. She was still confused. Was this happening, or was it all part of a weird dream?

"That's what you're choosing to focus on?" Evie practically shouted.

Upon closer inspection, Evie appeared close to hyperventilating. "Maybe we should go downstairs and get a glass of water," Grace said soothingly.

"I'll call Thorne," Rebekah whispered as Grace passed, her arms wrapped around a visibly shaking Evie.

"Thanks," Grace mouthed back.

Grace poured Evie a drink when they were seated safely in the kitchen. "Anyone else?" she looked at Cassie and Megan as she held up the glass.

Both women shook their heads. "Can you tell us what happened?" Grace asked Evie once she'd downed about half the cup.

"At first, I thought I was dreaming," she began. "I felt something on top of me, something with claws," a shiver ran through her as she remembered the event. "When I realized I was awake, and there really was something on me, I assumed Piper had somehow gotten into my room and was 'doughing' me, you know?"

Grace nodded, no stranger to waking up to that very scenario. "Piper was with me," she said gently.

"I know that now," she shivered again. "At the time, I decided to just go with it, so I tried to pet her, only the animal was too big to be a kitten. That's when I turned on the light and saw red eyes glowing at me. Naturally, I screamed and tried to jump out of bed, but my screaming scared him, and he tried to run, but his claws got caught in the blanket, so we sat there wrestling for a few minutes. It was the worst few minutes of my life," she cried. "I was so scared."

"Did he scratch or claw you?" Grace asked. Not wanting to cause any further alarm, she tried to sound nonchalant. Possums were not known to attack humans, but on the rare occasion when they did, they could transfer diseases.

Evie gave herself a once over. "Doesn't look like it."

Grace breathed a sigh of relief. "I bet it was the worst few minutes of his life, too," she joked.

The doorbell rang, followed by the sound of thunder on the stairs. "I've got it," Rebekah called out.

"That's probably Thorne," Grace reassured Evie. "I'm sure he'll get his sorted out in no time."

"I'd like to know how he got in there in the first place?" asked Cassie.

That was a great question. One that Grace would also like an answer to. Evie's room did not have access to the attic, it was too hot for the window to be open, and her door was usually closed, which made it unlikely it had slipped in from the hall. Even if that had been possible, how would it have gotten in the hall? In the twenty years Grace had lived there, she had never seen a wild animal in the house. "I'm sure Thorne will have an answer," she said more confidently than she felt.

"Doesn't it seem strange that there was a possum in the hotel, and now there's one at the house?" mused Cassie. "In Evie's room, specifically," she added.

"Are you implying that someone deliberately put the possum in Evie's room?" asked Grace.

Cassie shrugged. "Just seems weird, that's all."

"Who would do such a thing?" asked Grace. "Surely you don't think I would do something like that?"

"Of course not," Cassie reassured her. "But, there are others who might be interested in causing problems."

"For me or for Evie?" asked Grace. "Because I can't help but notice that I'm the one dealing with the fallout from these critters."

"Yeah, but think about it this way," she said. "If the hotel was sabotaged, the wedding guests would have nowhere to stay. That would certainly put a wrinkle in the plan, don't you think?"

"What would be the point of letting it loose in Evie's room, though?"

"I'm not sure about that one. Maybe it was meant to upset her into calling off the wedding? Maybe it was meant to do damage? Or maybe it was just meant to be obnoxious. Who knows."

The sound of footsteps on the stairs momentarily ended their speculation. "Did you get him?" Grace asked Thorne.

He held up a cage in response. "Poor little guy was so scared he decided to 'play dead.' Made it easy to scoop him up and into the cage."

"Is he going to be okay?" asked Evie. "I'm worried he may have gotten hurt in our struggle."

"I'll give him a once-over before I release him back into the wild," Thorne assured her.

"Any idea how he got in here?" asked Cassie.

Thorne pursed his lips as he shook his head. "That is a bit of a mystery. I checked for the usual access points but couldn't find any signs of entry."

"Is it possible he's one of the possums from the hotel?" asked Grace. They had always assumed there was more than one but could never find any others. She was starting to suspect someone else emptied the trap before they could.

"I mean—yeah," he stammered. "But that would mean someone can access both the hotel and the b&b. So unless you suspect someone you know, you have a major problem on your hands."

"To some extent, that's true," Grace said quickly, hoping to avoid any potential fear from her guests. "But, we've been working at the hotel for weeks now. Anyone could have come and gone while I worked without me knowing."

"And the house? Can people come and go here?"

"It would be a little harder to move around without someone noticing. And riskier, but yes, it is possible. They would have had to plant him there during the day, though. Is it possible for someone to do that without Evie noticing?"

Thorne tilted his head to the side. "If they placed him somewhere he couldn't be seen, such as under the bed or behind a dresser, then yes. Possums are nocturnal animals and tend to sleep during the day, so he would have remained hidden until he woke up and searched for food and water."

"What about cameras?" asked Cassie. "I thought I saw one by the front door?"

"Cole installed a couple around Easter. I'm not sure if he has them on during the day. There's so much activity around here the notifications would drive him crazy."

"Check anyway, just in case," replied Thorne. "Also, it might not be a bad idea to make a police report. Without video, there's not much we can prove, but it wouldn't hurt to have a paper trail, just in case."

Grace groaned at the thought of talking to Officer Smith again. They had called a truce but were still no one's definition of friends. Her attitude toward him wasn't fair; she was just still so mad that he hadn't taken her seriously when the events with Dot began around Easter. It shouldn't have taken Cole to get the man to do his job.

"Fine," Grace relented. "I'll talk to him after I talk to Cole."

"Glad to hear it," he nodded. "Now, if you ladies will excuse me, I'm off to care for this little guy."

"I'll walk you to the door," said Rebekah.

Grace looked at Evie, relieved to see she looked much calmer and relaxed. "Do you guys think you can go back to bed? It's still pretty early."

"I don't know," Evie replied. "The thought of returning to the crime scene is pretty unsettling."

"How about you stay with me?" said Cassie. "It'll be like old times," she said cheerfully.

Evie hugged her. "I was hoping you would offer," she replied.

"Good night, everyone," said Grace. She remained in the kitchen for a while, needing a moment to calm her nerves. "I hate to see what a bill for a nighttime house call is going to cost," she said when Rebekah entered the room.

"I wouldn't worry about it," she said. "One of the perks of dating a vet," she replied when Grace raised her brow.

"I'm not dating a vet," said Grace.

Rebekah looped her arm through Grace's and began to lead her toward the stairs. "Guess it's a good thing I am," she smirked.

***

Unable to go back to sleep, Grace got dressed and went to Cole's. He still had an hour and a half left until his alarm went off, so she slipped into bed beside him and snuggled up to his chest. She may be unable to sleep, but at least she could lie there and listen to his heartbeat. It was one of the few things she found that calmed her anxiety. And she was definitely feeling anxious after the events of the night.

The thought that someone was sneaking around the hotel and, worse yet, her home, without her knowing, was terrifying. That they were terrorizing one of her guests was even worse. It had shades of Dot written all over it, and she was tempted to call Ray down in Florida just to verify she was still there. Although, she much preferred Dot to some faceless unknown.

When the alarm went off, she woke up feeling groggy and out-of-sorts. "Hey," she said to Cole when he looked at her.

"When did you get her?" he asked.

"Around four."

"Everything okay?"

"You should have a cup of coffee before I answer that."

"Why?" he asked, concern in his voice.

"Trust me, okay?"

They got up and went to the kitchen, Cole quickly starting the coffee pot. "Okay, spill," he said.

"I said drink coffee, not make it," she protested.

"Grace," he warned. "We don't have time for this."

"We don't have time for anything."

"Is that what this is about? You came here at four o'clock in the morning to complain that we're not spending enough time together?" he asked, exasperated.

"No, I came here at four in the morning because I was awakened at three by Evie's screams. Someone put a possum in her room."

His look was so funny that she would have laughed if she weren't so stressed. "Are you saying someone broke in?"

"I don't think they broke in so much as they walked in when we were out. I don't lock the doors during the day when guests stay in case they need access when I'm not home," she explained. "Is there any chance the cameras have been recording over the last twenty-four hours?"

Cole ran a hand through his messy hair. "Unfortunately, no. I only turn the cameras on at night. I don't remember getting any notifications last night, but I can check just in case."

"Thanks; Thorne wants me to talk to Officer Smith. It would be nice if we had something to give him."

"Wait, you called Thorne instead of me?" there was hurt in his voice, maybe even a tiny hint of accusation.

"He's a vet, Cole. Trapping animals is literally part of his job."

"That's usually the job of animal control," he corrected.

"You didn't have a problem with it at the hotel," she shot back.

He took a deep breath and then pulled her into his arms. "You're right; I'm sorry. He was the right person to call; I just don't like the thought of you being in danger and not being there to protect you."

"I wasn't in danger," she reassured him. "Besides, I'm not the one who called him; Rebekah did. I was too busy trying to calm Evie down to think about calling anyone."

"Is she okay?"

"I think so. She was pretty shaken up, but she seemed better by the time everyone went back to bed."

She felt him nod against the top of her head. "I'll go to the police station with you after we finish the morning chores. But Grace, I think it's time to start locking those doors."

"Yeah, I agree, but who will let people in if I'm not there? Handing out keys seems like a worse plan than leaving the doors unlocked."

"At least lock the front door. Granny and Gladys will hear if someone comes in through the back. Best case, that deters any further break-ins. Worst case, someone enters, and they have to call the police."

"Worst case, someone enters and harms them before they can call the police," she said softly. So far, the possum could be considered a harmless prank. But what if this was only the beginning? The thought of Granny or Gladys getting hurt was too much to bear.

"I think we should make sure someone is at the house with them at all times, then," he said.

"How is that possible with the wedding in just a few days? I'll be back and forth between the house and hotel multiple times a day."

"I suppose Rebekah will be pretty busy as well?"

"As much, if not more so."

"Then Molly will have to work from home until the wedding is over."

"I'll talk to her," said Grace. "She might appreciate the opportunity to put her feet up while she works."

Cole made them each a to-go cup, then grabbed her hand and walked her to the barn. "You should take Max home with you when you go. No one will get past him."

"Are you sure? I know you'll miss him," she smiled.

"I'm sure," he kissed the tip of her nose. "Wait for me when you're finished. I want to be there when you talk to Officer Smith."

"Will do," she gave him a mock salute.

He rolled his eyes, then broke out in a grin. "See you soon."

"See you soon," she called back, but he was already too far away to hear.

Three

-Days till 4th of July-

The big day had finally arrived. For Grace, anyway. The day the guests checked in was always a big deal for her. It was like welcoming family. Even the ones who were challenging, after all, didn't everyone have that one difficult relative?

Cole and Grace spent the previous morning at the police station talking to Officer Smith. They had gone over the last night's camera footage, and, as predicted, there was nothing there. Since they had no evidence that a crime had occurred, as expected, there was nothing Officer Smith could do. This time, Grace wasn't mad at him. In the light of day, it was more likely that the possum had found a way into the house. The thought that someone was sneaking possums in and out of buildings was out there.

That had not stopped Cole from spending the night or making Max her constant companion. It also hadn't stopped Molly from staying home with Granny and Gladys. When Grace had told her what happened, she had agreed without hesitation, causing Grace to re-examine the uncharitable thoughts she'd been having about her friend as of late. Molly was not the source of her stress and anxiety; she would do well to remember that.

"Where you off to?" asked Evie.

"The hotel," Grace replied. "I have a few last-minute things to do, and then I plan to hang around and wait for Jake's relatives to arrive."

"I haven't seen the rooms since we painted last weekend. Can you believe an entire week has passed?"

Yes, she could believe it. "Just think, this time next week, you'll be officially married and on your honeymoon!"

"I know!" she squealed in excitement. "I feel like I've been waiting for this my whole life. Is that strange?"

"Not at all. If you want to stop by the hotel and give it a once-over, you're more than welcome. I'll be there till four."

"What happens at four?"

"At four, I'll come back here to start dinner. If you're concerned about someone being there, Rebekah will replace me until I return with the food. We'll serve dinner in the dining room at six, and then I'll stay till around ten in case someone arrives late."

"Sounds good. Thanks, Grace!"

"No problem." She finished setting breakfast on the breakfast bar, then grabbed her keys and purse. "See you later," she called out.

The hotel looked just as she'd left it the night before. Why that was a relief, she wasn't sure. Had she been expecting something different? If so, what? The incident with the possum had been unsettling, the thought that someone or someones had been in her home without her knowledge was pretty terrifying, but did that explain her unease, or was it something else?

Best guess, she was experiencing a case of the jitters. That always happened right before the guests arrived. It was that moment between she couldn't possibly do anymore and had she done enough to impress them.

Since she wasn't an expert in plumbing or electrical, she had no choice but to trust their hired experts. So far, everything worked as they claimed it would. All bathrooms had functioning sinks, toilets, and showers, and each room had its own window unit air conditioner, wired on its own circuit. John Langford had agreed to work up an estimate to rewire the entire building and hopefully would be able to start work in the next couple of weeks. For now, though, he had assured her the wiring was safe for her guests.

Inside, she decided to do a sweep of the building before she got started filling the mini-fridges. Starting at the top and working her way down, she checked each room for signs of use, human or animal. Not spotting anything noteworthy, she grabbed a luggage cart, leftover from the early days, and began to load it up with water bottles, an assorted mix of soft drinks, juice, crackers, chips, and granola bars. All the things she kept on hand and readily available for her guests at home.

Once that was done, she gave the rooms a quick once-over with the vacuum cleaner, fluffed the pillows a few times, and wiped down the surface areas. The only thing that would have made things better is if she had some kind of plant or floral arrangements for the rooms. A little something to freshen the rooms up. She glanced at her watch to see if she had time to run to the home improvement store in the next town over but ultimately decided that would be pushing it. Time-wise, it was getting to the point when people could arrive at any minute.

Taking her time to inspect as she went, she returned to the lobby and looked around. Here was a room that needed a floral arrangement. Something big and beautiful that would draw people's attention. She knew it was unlikely, but she decided to call the flower shop, just in case.

"Hi Linda," she said when the owner answered the phone. "I know this is last minute, but is there any way I could get an arrangement or two for the hotel?"

"Hey, Grace," she replied. "Does it matter what type of flowers?"

"Nope, I won't even complain about the size, although something large would be fabulous if you have it?"

"You're in luck," she said. "A customer just canceled an order. She wanted three centerpieces for a family barbecue she was supposed to host on the fourth, but plans fell through. The flowers are red and white, and blue. Is that okay?"

"It's perfect," Grace beamed. "Thank you so much; I'll be there in a few minutes to pick them up."

"I have a delivery going out in ten minutes; I can have my driver drop them off if that would be easier for you?"

"That would be great; thanks, Linda!"

"You're very welcome, Grace," she laughed as she hung up.

Ten minutes and one large tip for the driver later, she had three gorgeous flower arrangements, one for the lobby and two for the dining room. As predicted, they livened up the place, adding a touch of warmth and class. She must remember to talk to Linda about setting up an ongoing order for both here and the b&b. It was the little details people noticed, and she wanted to make sure she gave her guests plenty to remember them by.

***

Half of the rooms were full by the time four o'clock rolled around. Jake's family members were a colorful bunch. Full of laughter, always joking, and somewhat loud. Nothing at all like his mother, thank goodness. This was going to be a fun crowd.

"Hey," Rebekah said when she entered the lobby.

Grace was sitting behind the desk, her laptop open in front of her. She had a list of the guests that were supposed to arrive organized in a spreadsheet. Time of arrival and room number were entered by the ones who had already arrived. "Hey," she replied. "Let me show you how this works." She showed Rebekah, who was far more tech-savvy than her, how to record the entries.

"How are you deciding which guest gets which room?"

To make things easier on the guests, bathroom-wise, since they would have to share, Grace had decided to do ten rooms per floor instead of fifteen on the first and five on the second. "If they are older or have mobility issues, first floor. Second floor if they're young or get around well enough to handle stairs for a few days. I always ask first in case an issue isn't visible."

"I can handle that. When will you be back?"

"I'd like to be back no later than five forty-five so there's time to set up the buffet before they come down. Call me if you need anything."

Rebekah nodded her focus on the computer screen in front of her. "Do you mind if I make a few improvements?" she asked absentmindedly. "Not that you did a bad job," she added quickly. "It's just—"

"Go ahead," Grace cut her off. "Anything you can do to streamline the process will be much appreciated." Outside, Grace greeted a couple of newcomers on the way to her car. The casseroles would take about an hour to heat, and she needed at least as long to make the rice, beans, salad, and salsa. Throw in time to preheat the ovens, load the car, and run back and forth before her house and Gladys's, and she'd be lucky if she made it in time.

The first thing she noticed when she entered the garage was the silence. The fridge was not loud, per se, but it did make a consistent humming noise. A noise that was missing. Concerned, she ran to the refrigerator and opened the door, only to be immediately overcome by the smell of rotting food.

After quickly slamming the door shut, she looked to see that someone had unplugged the cord from the outlet. The plug couldn't have fallen out on its own, and no one she knew would have 'accidentally' unplugged it. No, this was a deliberate act of sabotage, of that she was sure.

Tears of frustration stung her eyes as she stumbled outside and over to the patio, where she sat down hard on one of the chairs. All that food is gone. What was she supposed to do now? She had over thirty hungry guests to feed and no food to feed them with. Not to mention all the money that was now lost. It was enough to make her want to scream.

Her phone rang as she sat there contemplating a solution to her problem. Seeing it was Rebekah, she answered despite not wanting to talk to anyone. "Hello," she sniffled.

"Grace? What's wrong?" she asked.

"Someone unplugged the fridge. All the food is rotten. No way to feed the guests," she stammered.

"I'll be there in a few minutes," came a muffled voice from her end.

"You can't leave; someone needs to be there to check in the guests."

"Molly's here; she said she'd take over."

There was a click, then silence. Grace looked at her phone in surprise, then put it back in her pocket. Minutes later, Rebekah came flying out the back door, stopping when she saw her in the chair.

"I looked all over the house for you," she exclaimed.

"I've been here the whole time," Grace mumbled.

"Well, let's go," she grabbed her arm and pulled her to her feet, dragging her across the yard to the car.

"Where are we going?"

"To the store." Grace looked at her blankly. "Come on, silly, we don't have time for this."

"It's too late," Grace sobbed as the weight of everything she had been doing came crashing down. "There's no time to remake the enchiladas. We're doomed."

"No, we're not. Thorne is on his way to start the grill, as is Cole," she pushed her into the passenger seat, buckling her in for good measure, then hurried around to the driver's side. "We will get enough hot dogs and hamburger meat to feed a small army."

"You really think this will work?"

"Oh yeah, who doesn't love a barbecue? We'll fill a couple of coolers with drinks, open some bags of chips, whip up some baked beans, and call it a night."

"What about dessert?"

"Was that in the fridge with the rest of the stuff?"

Grace nodded as fresh tears slid down her cheeks. She had spent days preparing all that food. Whoever did this was a monster.

"We'll see what the bakery has and grab whatever's available. It won't be as good as whatever you made, but it will do. A lot of those people haven't seen each other in ages. They're so excited to hang out and catch up, I doubt they'll even notice this was thrown together at the last minute."

"Thank you," Grace wiped her eyes and blew her nose. "I don't know what I would have done without you."

"You would have shaken it off and figured it out, just like you always do." They pulled into the parking lot. "Do I need to come around and help you out of the car, or are you good now?"

"I can manage," Grace smiled. It was strange having someone treat her like a toddler. In a way, it was comforting. She spent so much time caring for everyone else; it was nice having someone take care of her. Tears threatened to fall again, so she shrugged them off and got out. They had a lot of shopping to do in a short amount of time. "Let's do this."

Two

-Days till 4th of July-

The barbecue was a huge success. Thorne and Cole had manned two grills each, flipping burgers and hot dogs like pros. No one mentioned the store-bought cakes or pies. No one questioned if it was thrown together last minute; they were all too busy talking to even notice or care, just as Rebekah said they'd be. That meant one meal down, eight to go. With no food. Yay.

Luckily, breakfast was going to be easy. Bea and Addie had agreed to provide some scrambled eggs and pastries, respectively, so all Grace had to do was stop by and pick them up. She was supposed to help Bea in the kitchen, but she had taken pity on Grace when she heard the news and released her from duty. So, when you added the cereal, fruit, and toast to the eggs and pastries, they had a pretty impressive breakfast spread, if she did say so herself. Which she did.

"This looks amazing," said one of the guests. It wasn't one of the ones she had checked in, so she had yet to learn who the woman was.

"I'm glad you think so," Grace smiled at the woman.

"What's on the agenda for today?" asked the man beside her.

Grace froze like a deer in headlights. Why were they asking her? Was she supposed to entertain them? Had she forgotten that little tidbit, or had someone else forgotten to let her know? It was the Sunday before a holiday; any business that wasn't closed would be packed. "Um, let me check on that," she excused herself before they could see her panic.

Unsure of who to call, she decided to start with Molly. "Why are the guests asking me about entertainment for the day?" she asked without saying hello.

"What time is it?" Molly asked through a yawn.

She checked her watch. "Seven o'clock," she replied. Oh, most people were still asleep, weren't they? Well, too bad. She wasn't, and she desperately needed help.

Grant came on the line. "What's the problem?" he asked sleepily.

"The guests expect me to provide entertainment, but no one told me I was supposed to do that, so I am woefully unprepared," she rambled.

"I don't remember including entertainment in the booking. Jake or Evie must have mentioned something."

"Okay, great. What am I supposed to do?"

"I don't know; I'm not from here, remember?"

Grace rolled her eyes. "That's a cop-out, and you know it."

"Fine, but I really don't know what to say. Is there anywhere you can think to take them?"

"No, not at this short notice. Nor would I have any way of getting them there."

Molly got back on the phone. "How about a game day in the park? We could set up some volleyball nets, a couple of games of corn hole, badminton, things like that."

It was very short notice, but a few townspeople usually set up food stands at events held throughout the year. They might be able to come out and help. That would solve the lunch problem, effectively killing two birds with one stone. "I think that should work," she said, warming up to the idea. "Can you handle the trip to the store, or should I call Rebekah?"

"We'll take care of it," she yawned again. "Meet you at the park around ten?"

"Sounds good."

After a few phone calls, she lined up a barbecue truck, an ice cream stand, and a guy with a portable grill. He agreed to do bratwurst and sausage since they'd served hamburgers the night before. All grumbled at the short notice, but no one said no. Business opportunities didn't come around often in their neck of the woods.

Confident with their plan, she returned to the dining room and made her announcement. "That sounds good, hon," said a woman in her early sixties. "But after last night, I'm not sure I'm up for a day of fun in the sun. Especially in this heat."

Her face fell. "What happened last night?"

The woman looked away in embarrassment. "I may have dreamed it," she shook her head. "Never mind."

"If you're referring to the noises, I heard them too," said a young man in the back

"You did? Oh, thank goodness. I was afraid I was going senile."

"I heard them too," came another voice.

Pretty soon, the whole room admitted to hearing mysterious noises. "Could someone please describe what they heard?" Grace asked, clearly exasperated.

"It sounded like ghosts," said the first woman.

"Ghosts?" Grace asked in confusion. "What do ghosts sound like?"

"Well, let's see," the woman said thoughtfully. "I distinctly remember the sound of rattling chains. Of course, there was the usual woohoo sound."

"I heard a loud banging noise," said someone likely staying on the second floor. "Like someone was hitting a wooden spoon against a pan or something."

"Is this supposed to be part of our stay?" asked an elderly man. "Like we're in a haunted house or...."

The man did not look amused. "Not at all," she reassured him. "This is not a 'haunted hotel,' and I have no idea where these noises are coming from. I promise I will do everything I can to figure it out."

"In that case, I might be up for a few games after I've had a morning nap," said the woman.

The rest agreed, then left to rest after assuring her they would meet her in the lobby at noon. Breakfast was over, seven meals, and one ghostbusting event to go.

***

"What's the plan again?" Rebekah whispered.

Rebekah, Grace, Thorne, and Cole hid in the hotel's kitchen, along with Cole's dog, Max. Grace had informed them earlier of the guests' 'haunting experience,' and they'd made a plan to try to catch the 'ghosts' in the act. When you combined this with the incident with the possum and the one with the fridge, it was too many coincidences to ignore. Someone was trying to sabotage the wedding. Or Grace's business. Either way, it needed to stop.

"You and Thorne will hide in one of the bedrooms on the second floor while Cole and I do the same on the first. Whoever hears a noise first will do their best to trap the perpetrators," Grace explained. "Once we have them cornered, we can call Officer Smith."

"What are the chances this person is armed?" asked a nervous-sounding Thorne.

"Low to none," said Cole. "These 'pranks' are annoying, but there hasn't been any sign they were meant to harm someone."

"These days, you never know," he mumbled.

"No, you don't," Cole said, taking his concerns seriously. "If at any point you feel uncomfortable, call the police and lock yourselves in one of the rooms."

"Okay, you ready?" he asked Rebekah?"

Rebekah took his hand and led him up the back stairs to the second floor. The kitchen staff had a staircase between the floors, likely to expedite room service. Grace had discovered it by accident one day and hoped it had remained hidden from the intruder, though she expected it hadn't. It was one explanation for how someone managed to move around without detection.

Following their lead, Grace took Cole's hand and led him and Max to one of the rooms at the end of the first-floor hall. "How long do you think we'll have to wait?" he asked once they were safely inside.

"The guests said the noises started between eleven and midnight," she replied.

Cole checked his watch. "Looks like we've got at least an hour to wait," he sighed.

"At least we'll finally put an end to this," she snuggled up to him on the bed, careful not to get too comfortable lest they fell asleep.

"Who do you think it is?" he asked, curious to hear her answer.

"Honestly? I have no idea. It's got to be someone Evie, or we know. We didn't start having problems until a week before the wedding."

"I hate to say it, but all signs point to you being the target. Yes, the possum was put in Evie's room, but as the bride, she would have been a great target for someone trying to ruin your b&b business. Now they're trying to sabotage the hotel, on top of ruining all the food you made for the weekend. You are much more of a common denominator than Evie is."

"But who would do this to me? Dot is still in Florida, trust me, I checked, and last we knew, Valerie was stranded in the Ozarks. No one else hates me enough to do this to me. At least no one I know of."

Cole's arms tightened around her. "I don't know, darlin', but hopefully, we're about to find out."

The hour passed slowly; seconds felt like minutes, until finally, Max got up and walked to the door, emitting a low growling sound. Cole commanded him to stand down while he went to the door and pressed his ear against it to listen. Curious, Grace got up to do the same.

First came the sound of rattling chains, just as the guests had described. The sound was muted, loud enough to be heard but quiet enough to make you question if you'd actually heard it. Whoever was doing this was good. Then came the howling noises. These were far more amateur, like noises you would expect a kid to make wearing a sheet over his head.

Cole motioned for her to stay silent and slowly opened the door. She could only guess that his intent had been to sneak up behind the 'ghost,' but the person had maintained a watchful eye and took off running the second Cole stepped into the hallway. "Max, get him," he commanded the dog.

Grace watched intently as Max took off after the guy. She loved Max and trusted him with her life, but seeing the large, hundred-and-twenty-pound dog chase after the trespasser was terrifying. She never wanted to be on the receiving end of one of Cole's commands.

The poor guy lasted all of a second before Max tackled him to the ground. Despite the dog doing little more than sitting on the guy's back, he still screamed as if he were getting mauled by a bear. To be fair, she probably would have done the same thing.

Once Cole reached them, he called Max off and lifted the guy to his feet, shoving him up against the wall as he searched for weapons. Satisfied, he removed the Halloween mask the guy was wearing and revealed a sniveling and shivering Greg.

"Oh my gosh," Grace gasped. "You're the one pulling these pranks?"

"Please don't hurt me," he stammered. His eyes darted back and forth between Cole and Max as if he couldn't decide who to fear more.

"We've got one, too," Thorne said from the end of the hall. He was dragging an angry Shelley by the arm, Rebekah trailing behind.

"Wait, what?" Grace said in confused shock. "You two are in this together? But you're supposed to be getting a divorce."

"This is all Evie's fault," Shelley shouted. "We were so happy until she had to go and ruin it all."

"How is Evie getting married the cause of your unhappiness?" Grace asked, genuinely interested in hearing the answer. This was so ridiculous she was tempted to become a writer just so she could share it with the world.

"She was supposed to marry Greg," Shelley sulked.

"This makes no sense. Did she hit her head when you caught her," Grace asked Thorne.

He shook his head, just as confused as she was, though likely for a different reason.

"Look, it's not that complicated," she said sarcastically. "Greg and I were at our best when our relationship was secret. It was exciting, sexy, and taboo, the thrill of getting caught heightening our senses. Once we got married, all that disappeared, and our relationship became boring, stale, and predictable."

"You seem to have forgotten that Greg dumped Evie, not the other way around," Grace pointed out.

"I don't care; he only did that because he was momentarily overcome with emotion. Obviously, it's me he wants," she sniffed. "Don't judge us because we're different," she snarled.

"Oh, I'm judging you, alright. It wasn't enough to ruin your sister's wedding once; you're trying to do it a second time out of pure spite. The two of you deserve each other, and I seriously hope Jesse and Jessica end up raising those babies as far away from the two of you as possible."

"Whatever," Shelley rolled her eyes.

Rebekah, who Grace hadn't noticed leave, appeared with a couple of officers behind her. "That's them," she said, pointing to Greg and Shelly.

"What!" Shelley screamed. "You called the cops! How dare you!"

Officer Smith stepped forward and cuffed her, the other officer cuffing Greg and then taking his arm to lead him away. "I'm assuming you want to press charges?" he asked Grace.

"Yes, will it do any good?"

"We won't be able to prove anything beyond the incidents here, so...."

"So, no?"

"It'll depend on how the prosecutors feel, but don't be surprised if their families find a way to make this all disappear."

"Will there at least be a record?" she asked hopefully. She had lost a lot of time and money due to their shenanigans, and both families were the type who only responded when their wallets were affected.

"I'll make sure of it," he replied.

Grace looked at him through new eyes. Officer Smith wasn't so bad after all. Plus, as Rebekah said before, he was cute. And he had a noticeably bare ring finger, though that didn't necessarily mean he was single. Still, she knew someone who might be perfect for him. "Is he single?" Grace asked Cole.

"As far as I know, yes. Why?" he asked suspiciously.

"No reason," she looped her arm through Cole's. "You guys ready to go home?" she asked everyone.

All three of them nodded. "Who's going to tell Evie?" asked Thorne.

"Not it," Rebekah said quickly.

"Fine," Grace groaned. "I'll do it in the morning after breakfast. Unless someone beats me to it," she said hopefully.

"With Gladys around, you might just luck out," Rebekah laughed.

"One can only hope," she replied.

One

-Days till 4th of July-

Either the gossip mill had failed for the first time in history, or Shelley and Greg's families had already managed to cover up the events of the previous evening. Grace strongly suspected it was the latter; gossip this good would have spread like wildfire. They may have managed to keep the police from talking, but they couldn't stop her. The best part, they had it all on video. No amount of denials could trump video proof.

Unfortunately, that still meant Grace had to tell Evie. Since it was the day before her wedding, she felt terrible breaking the news but ultimately decided she deserved to know. "I have something to say," Grace announced to the room over breakfast.

All ten of them quit talking and turned to face her, giving her their undivided attention. "Last night, we discovered someone has been trying to sabotage the wedding," Grace said slowly. She winced when Evie's smile faded, replaced by a look of consternation. "We caught Greg and Shelley at the hotel trying to terrorize Jake's family. I'm sorry, Evie, but they've been behind everything, including the possum in your room and unplugging the fridge."

"That means they were likely the ones behind canceling the flowers, the DJ, and the tuxedo rentals, weren't they?" she sighed. "I blamed Gloria," she shook her head in embarrassment and shame.

"What I don't understand is why?" asked Cassie.

"That's harder to explain," replied Grace. "They blame Evie for their relationship falling apart."

"That's rich coming from those two," she said sarcastically.

"I agree, but people like them seem to live in a different reality than us."

"I need to find Gloria," Evie stood up so fast she toppled over.

"She's at the hotel," Grace informed her.

"The Red Brick Inn, right?"

"No, the hotel here in town."

"I thought you kicked her out?"

"We kicked her out of the b&b. Since she apologized, I agreed to let her stay at the hotel with her husband. Didn't see a reason not to," she shrugged.

"That was very kind of you. Do you think she's still there?"

"As far as I know. Some of the guests talked about going to an antique store about thirty minutes from here, but she didn't seem interested."

Evie nodded and left the room, leaving the rest of them in silence. "I've got to admit, that is not how I expected this conversation to go," Grace said out loud to no one in particular.

"Sounds like you two were in an episode of Scooby Doo last night," Megan said with a laugh.

"Rebekah was definitely the Daphne," Grace laughed along with her.

"And Thorne is definitely Fred," said Cassie.

"Hey! Cole is not Shaggy," Grace said in mock indignation.

"Wasn't that his dog?" Cassie raised her brow.

"In all seriousness," Megan interrupted. "It's good that you meddling kids caught Shelley and Greg before the wedding. Evie's been distraught since her fight with my mother. She thought their relationship had turned a corner and was devastated to think she was still trying to ruin the wedding."

"I wish I'd known about that," Grace said sympathetically. "I could have reassured her if I hadn't been too busy hiding all the fires from her."

"You were only trying to help," Cassie reassured her. "No one here blames you for trying not to stress out the bride. I, for one, appreciate it."

"You girls are going to have to tell me all about Shelley and Greg over our manicures," Megan informed them. "This sounds too crazy to be true."

If she only knew. Her work done, Grace left to figure out a lunch plan for the hotel gang. Rebekah had suggested sandwiches, but that felt plain and boring. Then, just when she needed it, inspiration hit. They could do a build-your-own pizza party. That way, lunch could double as an activity. It was brilliant! Plus, there was the added bonus of the guests making their own meals, which significantly reduced her load. All she had to do was shop for ingredients and haul the barbecues to the hotel.

Since it was a work day, her options for help were limited. Fortunately, luck was on her side when Officer Smith arrived in his personal pick-up truck. "Any chance I could get you to help me with something?" she asked sweetly.

"If you promise not to get mad at me when I tell you Greg and Shelley's parents got the charges dropped," he replied.

"Figured as much," she said dryly. "Those two wouldn't be anywhere near as bad if their parents stopped coddling them."

"They never would have turned out like that in the first place if they hadn't coddled them since birth. Kids need consequences. I don't think those two have ever faced consequences in their entire lives."

Grace pulled out her phone and texted Jenny to meet her with some pizza dough at the hotel. "It's hard to imagine Evie comes from the same family as Shelley."

"I've thought that too. Luckily, she's marrying out of it."

"If only it were that simple. Can you help me move those grills down to the hotel?" she pointed at the grills lined up by the deck.

"You'll hold up your end of the bargain?" When Grace nodded, he agreed.

Before long, they had all four of them in the back of his truck. If she had timed things right, they would arrive at the same time as Jenny. Apparently, she really did try to set up all her friends. Maybe she should leave the hotel business and become a matchmaker instead. That sounded more fun than spending the rest of her life cooking and cleaning up after strangers.

"If you guys don't mind," Grace said to Jenny and Officer Smith. "I need to run to the store real quick. Be right back," she winked at Jenny as she gave a quick, discrete nod toward the officer. When Jenny winked back, she knew her message had hit home. Now, all she had to was wait and see if she had another success on her hand. From the way things were looking, the answer was yes.

***

The pizza party had been a big hit. Jenny had offered to stay and help, and Officer Smith, whose first name she learned was Tim, had offered to man the grills. These two had lived and worked in the same town for years and had never met until today. It was crazy when you considered Jenny worked at the two most popular eating establishments in town. There must have been hundreds of near-misses over the years. She could say the same about her and Cole. The time just needed to be right.

As a thank you for saving her behind, Grace had agreed to help cater the rehearsal dinner. As a server, not a cook, thankfully. The hotel guests were not included since the dinner was for the wedding party and close family only. That meant Grace had to feed them before she left for the winery. Still angry over losing the casseroles she'd made, she decided to go with something simple and set up a taco bar. Not only was that easy to do, it allowed the guests to, once again, make their own food. For their after-dinner entertainment, she set them up with some board games, including everyone's favorite, Pictionary. This crowd was going to have a blast; she just knew it.

When she arrived at the winery, it was hard to believe she was in the same place. Large, white tents lined the lake in front of the pier. Round tables with white linen cloths were spread out underneath; twinkling white lights were strung in the trees creating a fairy-like atmosphere. An area for dancing had been set up to one side, while a couple of smaller tents were back a way, one for the bartender and one for the food. It would be even more spectacular the next night when the flowers were added, and music played.

She watched from the serving tent as Evie, Jake, and their wedding party went through the motions. When they agreed they were confident they knew what to do, they took seats at the tables, and Grace, Jenny, and a woman named Barb began to serve. Addie had outdone herself by choosing a 'miniature' theme. Sliders, mini corn on the cob, drumsticks, turnovers, pies that fit in your hand, crab cakes, lobster rolls, basically anything you could think of, only in miniature.

They were happily eating and chatting when the sound of metal on glass got their attention. "As the bride's parents," a tall man in a suit began. "We have something we'd like to say."

Grace looked around for someone to stop him, but everyone was frozen. Tempted to do something herself, she stood down when Evie got up and approached her parents. "No, I don't think you do," she said loudly enough for everyone to hear. "You said everything you needed to say when you stood by and allowed my sister to hijack my wedding day. You said everything you needed to say when you hosted her wedding to my former fiance at your home. And you said everything you needed to say when you accused me of being a selfish jerk for refusing to show up and allow you to humiliate me at said wedding. It's time for me to say something. You are not welcome at my wedding. You are not welcome in my home. You are not welcome in my life. Now, please spare us all the embarrassment of escorting you from the premises and leave."

"We're your parents," he said through gritted teeth.

"Says the man who literally just bailed Shelly out of trouble for trying to ruin my wedding. Again," she emphasized.

"You will regret this," Evie's mother said sharply. She grabbed onto her husband's arm. "Let's go," she told him.

The man pulled an envelope out of his inside jacket pocket. "I was going to give you this," he snarled. "But since I'm no longer family, I think I'll give it to your sister instead," he ripped up the check and tossed the pieces at her feet.

For her part, Evie remained calm, though Grace could see she was shaking. Jake stepped up behind her and laid a hand on her shoulder. "I think it's time you do as the lady asks," he told the pair.

With a final snarl, he turned to leave. "You'll regret this," he called over his shoulder.

Jake hugged Evie, shielding her from the horror-filled eyes of her friends and family. The crowd remained silent as Gloria approached. She put her hand on Evie's back, and to everyone's surprise, Evie turned and buried her head in her shoulder as huge sobs wracked her body.

"It'll be okay," she said, patting her back.

They stayed like that until the sobs subsided. Grace pulled a tissue packet from her purse and handed it to Evie. "Thanks," Evie tried to smile as she dried her tears.

"I'll make sure we have security set up tomorrow," Grace assured her.

"That's not your job," Evie said with a laugh.

"It is now." She retreated to the serving tent to make a few phone calls while Evie returned to her table. Conversation resumed, albeit in hushed tones, as people tried to make sense of what just happened. It took some time, but eventually, the atmosphere shifted back to its happier, pre-interruption time.

"We need to make sure that doesn't happen again," Addie told Grace.

"Already on it. I'm trying to find some guys who won't be bribed by the promise of money. Know anyone?"

"I may know a few," she said thoughtfully. "We should talk to Bea. If we can't come up with anyone, I know she can."

"Sounds good; I'll call after we're done."

"That poor child," Addie clucked her tongue. "I have a feeling her parents are headed for a downfall. People are only willing to look the other way for so long before they decide enough is enough."

"I wish it would have happened sooner." She told Addie about Greg and Shelley's recent exploits.

"They're even worse than we thought," she exclaimed. "Poor Evie."

"Poor Evie," Grace echoed. "Maybe she should have eloped."

Happy 4th of July!

"Hey there," Grace said to Jake. He was standing at the end of the pier, where he would soon be declared husband and wife with Evie. "Are you ready to put a permanent end to your bachelorhood?" she teased.

"I've been ready since the day I met her," he grinned. "What about you? I have a feeling you'll be next."

"No," Grace shook her head. "My money's on Emilio and Vanessa. It will be a while before Cole and I take the leap."

"How do you feel about that?"

"If it were up to me, we would already be married. But if this experience has taught me anything, I need to learn to be patient and enjoy the moment."

"That's a good lesson to learn," he agreed. "Not an easy one when it comes to matters of the heart, though."

No, it's not. But I spend so much time complaining about our lack of time together; I don't enjoy the time we do have together. I have this terrible habit of watching the clock and counting the minutes until he has to leave. It's a horrible way to live," she laughed.

"I do hope you get over that," he smiled. "By the way, I wanted to thank you for taking care of my family. They have been having a blast! More than a few have claimed this is the best vacation they've ever had."

"I'm not sure I'm buying that," she shook her head while smiling. "But I'm glad to hear it. Comments like that make it all worth it."

"I've heard about how difficult this has been for you. Was witness to a small part of your pain at the painting party."

"Yeah, but we made it. And now, I'm removing my hostess hat and putting on my guest hat. I'm officially in guest mode, baby!"

Jake laughed as they mimed clinking glasses. "You have definitely earned it," his smile faded slightly. "Do you think there'll be another incident like the one last night?"

"Nope. Bea, Addie, and I took care of that. Unless her family launches a full-scale attack, they won't get in here tonight."

"They have a lot of money...."

"That may matter to some but not to all. Trust me, Jake, you guys are safe."

Cole approached from behind, surprising her by grabbing her waist and lifting her off the ground. "You look beautiful," he whispered in her ear.

"Put me down, silly," Grace laughed. Her laughter died when she saw him in his suit. There wasn't a male model alive that could hold a candle to him. Even if she is biased. The look in his eyes showed her he knew exactly how he made her feel.

After a moment too long to be considered proper, he turned to face Jake and held out his hand. "Congratulations, man. Cheers to a long life together."

"I appreciate it," he shook Cole's hand. "You two enjoy your evening together. There's plenty of romance in the air," he grinned as he waved his hand around at the decorations.

Votive candles floated on the lake near the pier. White roses adorned the tables, the candles in the center producing a soft glow. As romance went, this would be tough to beat, and she was proud to have had a hand in bringing it to life.

They took their seats at a table with Conor, Emilio, Vanessa, Molly, Jake, Granny, and Gladys. It felt familiar, almost like any other day, only fancier. "Maybe I should set the breakfast table like this," Grace joked.

"That could be fun," said Gladys. "It would lose its luster after a while, though. Better to keep things like this for special occasions."

"Maybe every day should be special," Grace said thoughtfully.

"I won't argue with that," said Granny.

The wedding song began to play, putting an end to their conversation. They turned in unison to watch Evie walk from a nearby tent down to the pier where Jake waited. Cassie and Jake's brother, Ted, as their only attendants, stood to the side.

She was beautiful in her white, off-the-shoulder gown; her smile lit up her whole face. Not a single sign of fear or nervousness was present on her face, only love. Love that shined so bright it brought tears to Grace's eyes. Evie definitely should not have eloped. They deserved this moment.

Grace reached under the table and took Cole's hand. Some day she hoped they would have their moment, but for now, she was content to sit beside him and watch their friends have theirs. When Cole squeezed her hand, tingles ran up her arm. Out of the corner of her eye, she saw his lips quirk and knew he felt it too.

Mayor Allen, or in this case, Pastor Allen, began the ceremony. When he got to the part where he asked if there were any objections, the crowd held their breath, then let it out in a whoosh when none came. The bride and groom laughed, but their gaze never wavered.

Five minutes later, the ceremony was over, Evie and Jake officially pronounced husband and wife. Crazy how much time, effort, and money went into something over in twenty minutes or less. As they exited the pier, Evie stopped and took her bouquet back from Cassie. "I need all the single ladies to step forward," she called out.

Grace groaned in response. "She's going to do that now?" she asked. "I thought this was traditionally done after they served the cake?" Her plan had been to conveniently use the restroom when the time came, but that excuse was obviously not going to fly now.

"Come on, Grace," Vanessa grabbed her hand and dragged her along. "It'll be fun."

"It's so embarrassing," Grace whined. "If I don't try, people will think I don't want to marry Cole. If I do try, they'll think I'm desperate."

"You are putting way too much thought into this, girlfriend. Even women who aren't dating anyone want to catch the bouquet. It's like winning a prize, that's all."

"I guess," she mumbled. They assembled in a group of about twelve, clustered together so tightly Grace was afraid someone might lose an eye.

Evie counted down from ten, then tossed the bouquet over her shoulder. As Grace watched it fly through the air, a scream erupted as a woman in a white dress dove off a nearby table. "It's mine," she yelled as she crashed into the circle.

They stepped back to see Shelley on the ground, her hand wrapped firmly around the bouquet she had gone all world wrestling on them to 'catch.' Snatch was the more appropriate word, but hey, what are you supposed to do when something so crazy and unexpected happens before your eyes.

"Why are you wearing a wedding dress?" asked Grace.

"Because it's a wedding. Duh," she rolled her eyes as she sat up, clutching the bouquet in a death grip.

"Do I even want to know how you got in here?" asked Grace.

"Probably not."

"Then how about, why are you here?"

Shelley looked at her like she was dumber than a box of rocks. "I'm the sister of the bride. Really, Grace, I need you to keep up."

Evie and Jake recovered from their shock, or maybe it was laughter, who knew at this point and walked over. "I would like my bouquet back," Evie held out her hand.

"No, it's mine. I caught it fair and square."

"You're already married," said Evie. "Catching a bouquet before the divorce is final is bad luck."

Was that true? Grace had never heard that before; then again, she had never known anyone tacky enough to crash a wedding and turn into Ric Flair during the bouquet toss. Shelley didn't seem to be buying it either.

"Are you lying?" she asked, her eyes narrowed.

"Nope, ask around; all the older ladies know."

"Fine, take your stupid bouquet back," she thrust it back into Evie's hand. "I'm still getting married next. The bouquet means nothing," she screamed so everyone could hear.

Wyatt and Kenzie showed up in their golf cart. "We need you to come with us," they told Shelley. They grabbed her arms, gently pushed her onto the back of the cart, and drove away before she could make a scene. Well, more of a scene.

"Okay, ladies, one more time," Evie said.

They gathered together again, this time with more room between them. When Evie tossed the bouquet, it landed straight in Grace's arms. Stunned, she stared down at it, wondering what it meant. The women cheered and congratulated her as she smiled and looked for a way to escape. Some people were just not made to be the center of attention. Grace was one of them.

When she returned to the table, she avoided Cole's eyes, too embarrassed to see what she assumed would be fear, concern, disgust, or some combination of the three. To her relief, Rebekah offered to take the bouquet and wrap it up, storing it away for safekeeping. Grace gladly handed it over, hopeful the reminder of what it stood for would disappear along with it.

Dinner was served as everyone chattered around her. She did her best to go through the motions, but the night was bittersweet. Her friends were married and about to start their life together. And she was obsessing about a stupid bouquet and breaking her promise to herself to live in the moment.

The cake was a delicious vanilla with fresh strawberries and blueberries in honor of the holiday. As the last of the guests finished, Jake stood up and clinked his glass. "First of all, thank you for coming out and sharing this special occasion with us," he said to a round of cheers. "Second, I would like to invite all of you to join us by the lake."

Jake led Evie, who looked as surprised as everyone else, through the tent and over the lake's edge. When the last person made their way over, a loud boom shattered the silence, followed by a burst of color in the dark, clear sky.

Grace stared in awe up at the sky. This was the one thing they had forgotten to plan, yet it was a perfect way to end a perfect day. "Do you like them?" Cole asked softly.

"They're beautiful," she replied, her eyes never leaving the sky. It was stupid, but she still couldn't look at him, even when he wrapped his arms around her waist and pulled her back against his chest.

"Not as beautiful as you," he whispered in her ear.

She leaned her head back against his shoulder, her heels high enough to bridge part of the gap in their height difference.

"I love you," she whispered back.

"Want to tell me why you've been avoiding me?"

"I caught the bouquet," she answered. The burst of color momentarily illuminated their faces. Both showed concern, albeit for different reasons.

"Are you afraid I'm going to throw you over my shoulder and carry you off to the nearest preacher?" he teased.

"More afraid you'll go screaming off into the night in the opposite direction."

"Never going to happen," he kissed the spot just behind her ear, chuckling when it sent a shiver through her body.

"You're wrong for that," she whispered huskily.

"Am I?" he kissed her again, his arms tightening around her waist.

"I'm pretty certain most people would consider this indecent," she wrapped her arms around his neck, desperately attempting to pull his lips down to hers.

"Hmm," he moved them into the shadows. When he was sure no one could see them or was paying attention, he gave in and kissed her.

They swayed gently to music only they could hear, lost in each other's embrace as the others oohed and ahhed around them. Even surrounded by dozens of people, it felt like they were only two people in the world. "Would it be tacky to leave early?" she asked between kisses.

"I doubt anyone would notice," he assured her.

"Then maybe we should get out of here while we still have a chance."

Half a dozen kisses later, they held hands while trying to slip away from the lake unnoticed as they rushed to Cole's truck. On the way, they ran into Evie and Jake, who appeared to have the same idea. "You never saw us," they all said in unison.

They laughed, then ran the rest of the way to their trucks. "Please tell me you're free for the rest of the night," Cole said, kissing her again before starting the engine.

"I'm all yours," she snuggled up against him, eager to maintain their closeness as they made the twenty-minute drive back to his place.

"Home?" he asked.

"Home," she agreed.

Afterword

Dear Reader,

Thank you so much for reading *Countdown to 4th of July*! As someone who lives in a small town, it's fun writing about the dynamics. Some are, of course, dramatized for storyline purposes, but a lot are pretty accurate. Restaurants are the best places to go if you want to know what's going on. Gossip spreads like wildfire, especially if it's scandalous or involves someone from a well-known family. And people will stop to help you if you appear to need it. Honestly, there is nowhere I would rather live.

Next up will be, Countdown to Halloween! I absolutely love Halloween, so I am really looking forward to this one. It's about time for Molly to have her baby, the hotel is getting close to officially opening for business, and there will be a new group of guests to get to know and love.

To preview or purchase the next book, and experience more of Winterwood, check out <u>holidaycountdownbooks.com</u>or search for the holidaycountdownseries on amazon.com.

Happy Reading!

-Dianna

About the author

Dianna is a wife, mother, reader, writer, and small-town girl at heart. She resides in a rural Missouri town of less than twenty-five hundred people with her husband and three boys in a late 1800s home they've been lovingly restoring when she isn't busy working on her next book.

A romantic at heart, she believes in happily-ever-afters rooted in realism and, most importantly, humor!

She is the author of Forsaking the Dark, a paranormal romance, The Queen's Revenge, a historical romance, and the Holiday Countdown Series, a sweet, small-town romance series.

Made in United States
Cleveland, OH
16 June 2025